Homegirl!

Ryder Collins

Homegirl!
by Ryder Collins
Honest Publishing

Manufactured in the United Kingdom
Cover: Nick Thompson

To all the punkboys & homegirls out there... yo.

Big thanks to my editors – Chris, Bogdan, and Daniel, for believing in and caring about *Homegirl!* so much you wouldn't let me get away with any shit. To all the womens that gave me abortifacient facts, thank you for sharing things the Man don't wants us to know ... To my fam and friends, thanks for giving me the time and space while I lived through/about *Homegirl!* & to the editors of *Sleep. Snort. Fuck.*, *The Meth Lab*, *Bastards and Whores*, *Juked*, *Fix It Broken*, and *Freaky Fountain Press* thank you for publishing pieces of *Homegirl!* before she was even done.

ONE

It's not that she was at a crossroads in her life, cos she wasn't. Not really.

Homegirl got the café job about the same time she'd decided to give college another try. She got the café job cos not only was she young and lithe and hot and rocked brown platform boots and short skirts and attitude, but she also was kinda friends with someone who worked at one of the owners' other hip-urban-grungy-punky moneymakers; she decided to give college another try cos she thought she didn't want to work food service all her life.

Duh. Stick to food service; real grown up jobs are dull and disappointing.

She also had this vague notion that she wanted to be a writer. The vague notion hovered at the corner of her vision; she sometimes and hazily saw herself as one of those hip writers who wrote in a café and wore cool boots and scarves and vintage looking clothes that were actually new, one of those hip urbane writers everyone knew and who could get wasted and pee on the hors d'oeuvres table at the party and kiss all the girls' boyfriends and all the boys' girlfriends and all the king's men and get naked and scream about how pronouns and adverbs are destroying the very fabric of our existence by keeping us all separate and negating the very actualities that constitute existence or some such bullshit and everyone would just say, Oh, that Homegirl. She's a writer. Famous, you know. That's how those writers do.

But, instead of being the famous writer writing in the café, Homegirl was the café girl waiting on or cooking for the someday famous writer in the café.

Stupid Homegirl, don't she know the café girls can't play?

Girls can't get wasted like that cos girls will be mommies. Girls will be mommies and they will take care of the chilluns. Girls will be mommies and they don't carry their own pens like boys. They best they can do is plop out big blood clots once a month, but that's just gross cos you can't write your name in menstrual blood in the snow, not without an instrument or something. & that doesn't count.

Homegirl also had this vague notion that you had to go to school to become a writer.

Sucker.

You gots to live it, is what you gots to do.

Homegirl tries to do both, live and learn, and when she's living it takes her very long to learn and when she's learning sometimes she forgets to live. It is a conundrum, especially cos for Homegirl real living involves the sexing and the drinking and the naughtiness of food service and she doesn't always learn from the live-living things she does and so she does them again and again and again and again, and learning involves going to school and listening to teacher and reading the readings and taking crap core classes about rain and snow and the maths and linguistics with elementary ed majors who are all women and not cute and some even wear bows in their hair still – really, who does that?, and all these womens like the chilluns and care about the future of our society in terms of manners and etiquette and alphabets and numbers and rules and regulations and minding ps and qs and Hallmark cards and chicken soup for the fucking soul and tight-laced Protestant church services and cute-cloying life lessons learned in kindergarten.

In kindergarten, Homegirl'd learned two things: (1) she was afraid of those bigger than her, and (2) she just didn't fit in.

She learned to hide her fear by flirting with or just fucking (1).

& some of them are big/tall motherfuckers, cos Homegirl, in her high heeled boots, can reach 6'.

As for (2), she tried, man, she tried for as hard and for as long as she could.

TWO

Of all her boyfriends or pseudo-boyfriends or even friends, Homegirl liked to hang at Punkboy's house the most. For a dirty punk rock boy covered in tatts who didn't like deodorant and who could smell either surprisingly sexy or really really bad when sweaty, Punkboy's house was extremely well-maintained. Punkboy's dirty little secret was that he was a domestic punk rocker; he didn't let many people over. If he was stoned/drunk enough, though, he'd make Homegirl breakfast or even every now and then a late dinner. She'd watch him cook and wish she had a long flowy gauzy skirt on so she could re-enact that scene from *Sid and Nancy*.

I look like fucking Stevie Nicks!

Homegirl wanted someone to love her so much they could suicide together. She wanted love that was crazy and fucked up. Love that would travel all the way across the country hopping trains just to be with her. Love that would steal baby rabbits from pet stores and then brain them for attention, and love that would leave French bread and brie or Tofutti and tampons on her doorstep. Love that would hide books written just for her in her drawers for her to find later. Love that would actually hide in her drawers and spy on her or just fondle her panties because love couldn't be far from her, but didn't want to scare her too much.

She wanted to die fucking; it would be the only way to go.

But, all Homegirl had at the moment were the laissez-faire

Punkboy and the laissez-fairer Richboy, and neither of them left anything on her doorstep.

One night Punkboy and she'd come back to his house from the dive bar; Punkboy lived conveniently down the street and didn't drive at all, didn't even have a license and got around on fixies and skateboards and his own two feet, so it was also good for Homegirl cos then she didn't have to drive drunk; although she'd drive drunk if there was even the hint of a hard cock at the end. She'd sat at his 50s resale formica kitchen table as he made some primavera with fresh veggies even. He served it with tallboys of PBR, of course, and they ate it all up, smacking drunkenly.

Usually, Homegirl tried very hard not to eat around people she was fucking or even people she was fucking attracted to. She felt like it took some of her mystery away. Made her more real and less desirable. It made her vulnerable, more vulnerable than giving head, which also made her feel vulnerable and self-conscious, and she'd hide this by deep-throating any guy she wanted and some she didn't. Homegirl also didn't like to eat in public. She didn't care around Punkboy; she felt like she could do pretty much anything around him. She even let him watch her shit every now and then. It turned him on. He liked to give rim jobs.

She'd never eaten let alone shat around Richboy.

After the primavera, Punkboy'd served cheesecake with cherry pie filling on top. Cos Homegirl was still so drunk, she tipped the plate onto herself as she tried to grab it from Punkboy's tattooed hands. She was always always turned on by tattooed hands, but you've probably all guessed that

7

already. She wiped the cake off with the paper towel she'd used as a napkin. Then she got up, clutching her stomach over the big red stain.

I'm dying; they got me, she kept saying and giggling. She thought it was pretty fucking hi-larious. She backed herself up against the wall and slid down it. Avenge me, she gasped and then convulsed, long legs splayed out in a vee.

Punkboy stared into her vee, snorted and then said, If you're dead, I get the last Pabst.

Homegirl got her ass up right quick and said, I'll fight ya for it. Then they were wrestling and you know what drunken wrestling often leads to.

At least I hope you do.

& if you don't, I feel sorry for you, that you've lived a life so far and you're getting older older older and never engaged in drunken wrestling or, worse, the glimmer of drunken wrestling's never even shone in your eye. That no punker's let you into their home and made you drunken pasta or sexted you or rubbed you raw with tatted fingers. That you've never smelled food service sweat and got turned on or that you never wanted to wear gauze or be around someone wearing gauze ironically or that you've never grabbed and tousled and then licked that food service sex sweat away all night into morning and back to the darkness again.

When Punkboy cooked, Homegirl could pretend they were a couple for reals. That this was how it was every day. Punkboy cooking; Homegirl watching, drinking, talking, listening, sharing.

Even in her imagination, Homegirl ended up getting

wasted, drinking wine as Punkboy cooked. In her domestic fantasy, Punkboy never grabbed her and spanked her with that chartreuse spatula she was always eyeing. He never spontaneously threw her up on the counter and started eating her out. Even in her fantasy, Homegirl was bored with the routine and left without saying good-bye early one morning.

But making her foods and sexting her was the most commitment Homegirl'd gotten from Punkboy so far, so Homegirl wasn't bored, and they'd been hitting it for almost three years on and off.

They'd met at the café they both worked at; Punkboy was the only one of three dudes she worked with on her first nights who'd even talked to her.

She should have known it wasn't because he was a nice guy.

He had texted her the sweetest thing anyone'd ever said/ texted her, tho, just recently. *I have been thinking about your pussy every day.* She thought it so endearing that it was so grammatically correct.

This was a few months back when they hadn't been hanging out regularly. To put it more simply, they'd been off. He'd had a girlfriend and Homegirl'd kinda been seeing this other "nice guy" who wanted to be a pediatrician, a proposition that made Homegirl's clit want to jump back in its hood and hide every time his little fingers or littler wiener got near it.

Homegirl'd texted back, *Just shaved my pussy and did some other things in the shower. Left ya a landing strip so you'd know where to put it.*

That was as close to love as Homegirl got.

THREE

Homegirl was better off without either of them, Punkboy or Richboy, probably, but every time she decided to leave them alone they'd call or text or FB her something and she'd be off just like that to hang out. There's no simile here to describe the immediacy of her reaction, even crack rock don't do.

She'd met the one in her writing workshop – a rich anarchist, and the other at work – a punk anarchist. Both of them liked to fuck. A lot.

So did Homegirl.

Neither of them, punker and rich guy, are anarchists, really. Homegirl's just fascinated by, almost obsessed with, those G20 anarchist protestors. Or maybe I am. No, it's Homegirl; she's the one who has fantasies of being grabbed and fucked from behind by a corporate-hating, window-smashing, black-balaclavaed freegan anarchist. I don't. Really.

Homegirl did the rich elitist in her car. It was their fifth time, not that Homegirl kept count, well, yeah, she did in the beginning of a fling or relationship or whatever; the others'd been at his house. They'd done it in her car or tried to do it in her car this time cos they were coming from some workshop bar get-together and he only had a moped, a souped-up Italian moped, some hipster brand Homegirl couldn't remember. While they were making out in the front seat of her hatchback, rich anarchist'd pinned her down and started pulling her hair hard and this *before* penetration. Then he was biting her all over, and then he pulled her panties down and moved his cock in very slowly. She liked it and wanted more and said so. He started pinching and slapping her and pulled out without coming, without even getting his dick very wet or very far in.

Last time he'd said, You got a tight little snatch, natch, and then slapped her ass, which she liked cos it was sexy and naughty and cos she allowed it. This time all he said was, I'm done, and wouldn't say any more. He went catatonic almost. Homegirl was kind of worried about him and trying not to be pissed. Maybe he wasn't such an asshole cos the other time they'd had all right sex. At least he'd finished. Maybe this time he'd had too much drink or a combo of drugs + alcohol or just a combo of drugs with a couple of beers as a topper. Homegirl was naïve in a hard kind of way and that was the worst way ever to be naïve.

She thought she was safe from naivety cos she was hard, but that made her even more susceptible to naivety. She knew people were bad and she knew the bad things they could do because she was bad herself. But, she was bad only in a very little way. She didn't always realize there were people way way worse than her. And those people usually had agendas. Homegirl was only bad spontaneously.

Homegirl drove him back to his flat cos she thought he'd never make it back on his souped-up mopeddy thing. She was starting to believe it was all just because he was really fucked up on something. She watched him as he took his long-legged time going up his steps and tried not to think he was doing

11

it on purpose, torturing her for no reason. *Look at these legs, bitch. You could've been straddling them. We could've been doing things together but you fucked it up.*

Homegirl was still wet and only very partially fucked.

She went where she thought the punk-anarchist might be. She went where she knew where her punk rocker would be.

The dive bar.

They did it in the bathroom then, of course. The bathroom had no lock on it but they didn't care; Homegirl wanted to be a writer, like I said, and punk rock boy was as close to nihilistic as most blue collar Miltown guys got.

Writers keep themselves open to all sorts of experiences, or at least that's what I'm told. And, need I say? Nihilists just don't fucking care.

Homegirl always carries a black notebook as proof of wanting to be a writer. It's a moleskine she stole from Richboy's flat. He had a bunch lying around his bedroom and when he left to go piss after they'd fucked the last time successfully, Homegirl'd scooped this one up and put it in her big pleather bag. The notebook was only very slightly used; it had a sketch of Richboy naked and he looked elven and someone had given him wings. Probably one of his other girls, cos it was signed *Because I'll always love you but I'm looking for that heart of gold, Happygirl.* And Happygirl was outlined in a big golden glitterpen heart, and Homegirl not only couldn't appreciate the Neil Young reference cos her parents were fans and thoughts of them slow-dancing to *After the Gold Rush* made her gag, but she also didn't know or care to know who the fuck Happygirl was so she ripped out and burnt up that hipster ironic shit in her bathroom sink after her roommates went to bed. Plus, who the fuck did Happygirl think she was that she'd find that heart of gold? No one Homegirl knew ever had, which was why Homegirl kept looking cos she'd always rooted for underdogs and other fucked-up thingies, like Trotsky.

Homegirl'd had a huge crush on Trotsky in the 5th grade and thought it so romantic and über-dashing he'd gotten an icepick to the head.

After having sex with Punkboy in the dive bar bathroom, and that was hot and Homegirl got off, thank god, Homegirl pulled out that moleskine at the bar and wrote, *The only thing the nihilist woman cares about is the cock.* She changed it a sec later to *Cos the only thing the nihilist hetero-woman cares about is the cock.* Then she looked at Punkboy but he was busy staring at his tallboy of PBR. Homegirl looked back at her notebook and corrections and wondered when she'd got so p.c. and/or who she was trying to impress. Plus, deep down, well not even that deep really, she knew she wasn't a nihilist.

Homegirl's awkward like that, tho. She envies Punkboy his punkdom, his teen years spent in squats fighting the Man by listening to visiting hardcore bands and flirting with dirty punk braless girls. Punkboy's ease with himself and his cock and his PBRs. She envies Richboy his ease, too, his ability to sidle up to anyone or better even, to be aloof and have everyone come to him. He's super tall, good-looking, well dressed, and everyone says he's hot. Punkboy's not super tall or super good-looking and def not well-dressed, but he does a-ight looks-wise and he's wiry as fuck and can pick Homegirl up when they fuck. Homegirl's tall, good-looking, and well-dressed, too, but she thrifts cos she has to, and Homegirl's hot but it takes a certain brave soul to acknowledge it cos she don't look like everyone else. She's exotic and erotic. A lot of men want to fuck her but don't know why and can't be bothered to figure it out either.

She's just too much work and not in a high maintenance kinda way. Men think she's crazy cos she likes to do her own thing and she likes to fuck; they think she's crazy but not crazy enough. They want the crazy nagging kitchen laundry chilluns toilet cleaning woman, not the bedroom love crazy woman. Even tho they pretend that's what they're longing for all along.

Homegirl's not a classic beauty, but she is. Her face is, but she don't act like it. She doesn't let her face rest; she doesn't wear enough or the right kind of make-up; she makes funny faces; she worries too much about stuff. Stupid class stuff, especially. Probly cos she grew up in the suburbs, rejecting and rejected all at the same time. That's why she lets Richboy get away with so much shit.

She knows this but doesn't really know it yet.

FOUR

Although Homegirl met Punkboy before Richboy, Homegirl didn't get Punkboy's intentions right away, like I said; she got Richboy's or maybe she tried to make her own intentions Richboy's, maybe he'd had no intentions towards her, maybe she wasn't even on his radar.

Yeah, right, that's why Richboy wrote those stories about her in workshop. That's why every time they were together at a bar with their workshop, cos their prof was a bored bored man, and only alcohol could get him through the tedium of most of their stories, oh yes, I know, so he'd moved the class to a bar somewhat near campus, Richboy found a way to get her alone and corner her and press her up against a wall and he was goddamned tall and he boxed her in with his arms and it was so hot and Homegirl wanted him to fuck her right there up against the bar wall in front of the lameass people from their workshop and their lameass balding prof with the fake British accent, it's real, really!, but all Richboy did was ask her if she wanted a cigarette. Each and every time. & each and every time she would say yes in a small breathy voice she didn't even know she possessed and he would let one of his long gangly arms fall to his pocket and he would pull out a Camel. Sometimes, he would let both arms fall, but he'd still block her way with his long lean body and he'd pull out a pouch of Drum or Top and have her hold the pouch while he rolled her a cigarette and he was so close to her and she could feel his warmth and hear him breathe and smell his not-so-clean scent and see the oil in his hair near his brow and she wanted to lick that oil away and she wanted to put her mouth on his nose and suck in his breathing out and she wanted to grab his hands and put them on her breasts and her chest and collar bone and then neck and she wanted to straddle him and have him in her up against that fucking wall.

She almost loved that fucking wall. It was always the same wall, or one that looked very much like it.

But this was about Punkboy and how Punkboy was always nicey-nice to her and trained her in the kitchen at the café and answered her questions and made her vegan sandwiches even tho it went against every fucking fiber of his being not to put some kind of dairy or meat on that bread. The worst was when she asked him for a vegan wasabi.

You sure, he said.

Yeah, she said.

It'll be veggies and wasabi on bread, he said.

Yum, she said.

He liked her even more, especially after he'd added a huge wad of extra wasabi cos he had to compensate for the sordid non-meat-non-dairiness of the thing & she ate it all up anyway. He liked a chick that could take it all in, that could take heat on top of it.

He asked her out that very night and it was a group date thing, cos it was going to the bar after work with the two guys who were working counter and barely said hi to Homegirl cos one was engaged and the other thought he was the hottest fucking thing on the planet even beyond toast even beyond grilled cheese beyond bread boxes and beyond shaved pussies and money shots, he was hot and bald and had Egyptian tattoos as sleeves, but, c'mon, get over yourself; Homegirl's hot, too.

They went to the bar and they sat in a row, Engagedguy, Egyptiantatts, Homegirl, and Punkboy. Engagedguy and Egyptiantatts'd rode their motorcycles over while Punkboy'd walked his fixie besides Homegirl the ten blocks to the dive bar, and Punkboy'd thought about kissing her the whole way. First, he thought, I will kiss her on the end of this block. Then he thought, I will kiss her on the top of this hill. Then, I will kiss her after pointing out the house I used to rent that's now owned by a po. Then, I will kiss her when we get within two blocks of the bar. Then, I will kiss her if a hoopdie goes by bumping its system. Then, I will kiss her if a hoopdie prowls by quiet as sin. Then, I will kiss her before we get into sight of the bar. Then, when I can see the bar. Then, before we walk into the bar.

He didn't, but he told her to wait as he locked up his bike, then opened the door for her to the bar.

That was more than enough for Homegirl, the holding open of the door for her, but she didn't tell Punkboy that. If he'd pursued it that night, she would have gone home with him, cos she kinda had a feeling about him way down deep.

& those are the feelings more people should listen to.

I'm just saying.

But Punkboy didn't pursue it that night.

& Egyptiantatts did.

& Homegirl and Etatts were a secret couple for a while.

But, just a couple of weeks; Etatts loved himself way too much.

& they weren't that secret cos Punkboy knew. & Punkboy was pissed.

At both of them.

It took him a long time to get over it.

About two years, maybe more. But, this was supposed to be about Homegirl and Punkboy and how they got together.

After the failed group date, they made out a couple months later. Punkboy was walking Homegirl home from the café's yearly Labor Day picnic and they were wasted and they were standing on top of that hill where Punkboy'd wanted to kiss Homegirl at before and it was still warm outside and quiet, the hoopdies were prowling like sin, and it was perfect and they kissed with tongue and didn't bite, at first, it was gentle gentle as they got to know each other's tongues, as they felt the slippery twistings and turnings, and then they were biting and teeth meeting and clicking hungry but not in a bad way and there was some scratching and pressing and panting and then they decided to go to the bar where they met up with their co-workers and pretended like the make-out on the hill'd never happened.

They pretended for a while.

Punkboy started dating another chick from the café and Homegirl took up with this younger guy who'd just gotten hired and she started feeling some things for him and then she went to Montreal with a friend for a quick vay-cay and when she got back Youngboy was dating someone else and Homegirl was pissed and pretended like she didn't care about

Youngboy and his little bitch and Punkboy and his.

That weekend, tho, she went out to the dive bar Punkboy hung out at and he was there and Etatts was there and Engagedboy and her fave bartender was bartending and Etatts and her fave bartender were now roommates and they decided to have an afterbar and Homegirl had nowhere to go but home so she went to the afterbar and Punkboy had nowhere to be except his girlfriend's bed so he went to the afterbar and Etatts and Favetender lived there and Engagedboy went home cos he knew better. Some other people were there when Homegirl showed up with one of her convenient girlfriends and she ditched her girlfriend in the living room and her friend didn't notice cos she was concentrating on the bong that was going around and all of a sudden Punkboy and Homegirl were in the dirty months-o-afterbars kitchen surrounded by empty bottles and mountains of empty PBR tallboys and six pack rings (the floor was a bird's nightmare) and twelve pack boxes and they were alone and they were kissing again like they were at the top of that hill and they were careening among the bottles and kissing and they were whirling and waltzing and groping and kissing in the skeezy afterbar kitchen and they didn't notice the dirt or that the trash and bottles were being knocked around, sent spinning wildly, and mountains were crashing and Punkboy said, You wanna go?

FIVE

We all love our dichotomies so I'm gonna dichotomize the fuck out of this motherfucker. Woot. So, of course, I gots to follow that shit up with how Homegirl met her Richboy...

& Homegirl'd been kinda nervous to go to class; it'd be her first writing workshop ever and she didn't really know what to expect and what if they were all cool literati types who read cool underground scenesters she never heard of or those difficult texts like motherfucking Pynchon that she'd tried and put down. She'd gotten through *Gravity's Rainbow* halfway twice; she may have stopped at the same exact point both times.

So, Homegirl hadn't shown up late to class, but she definitely hadn't gotten there early. The class started at 6:30 and ended at 9:10. One day a week. Every Tuesday, which was a good night cos then she'd never be tempted to go to import night at the bar Labretboy hung at cos it'd be way too packed by the time she got there and even tho she and Labretboy'd broken up the last time almost a year ago there was no telling what would happen if the both of them were drunk and single in each other's vicinity; they were still on each other's radars. She knew this; she knew she should stay away from him and she had and she was so proud of her willpower but she knew it was tenuous at times cos he had a big Italian cock, which made her make noises that, according to his roommates, sounded like someone was killing her.

They drove each other crazy, in the sexy good way and in the fighting bad way.

Learning how to write would keep Homegirl out of trouble.

All of you that appreciate dramatic irony are probably having a good chuckle, washed down with a good Scotch perhaps, or maybe a Budweiser, hey – I don't know *you* yet, either, right now.

Homegirl got there at 6:27 and walked around the 4 rectangular pushed together tables that made up one big table that took up most of the classroom, scooting behind her classmates. She grabbed a seat at the corner of the big table furthest from the door and the head of the table, where the prof would probably sit. There was an empty space next to her and an old lady in the space after that. There were several old ladies in the class and a couple old guys and one really short guy and a guy in an unironic Slayer tee and some boring looking peoples, and no one looked literary except maybe the old lady with the reading glasses and the scarf but she looked a little more librarian than literati.

The prof walked in; he was short and balding and not attractive or very literary looking either.

Homegirl knew she was the hottest person in the room. Homegirl felt good about this and she also felt kind of shallow. Sometimes she wished she wasn't so physically and visually oriented; sometimes she felt like a guy. Girls were supposed to fall for personality, not looks, but Homegirl'd go with the hot asshole over the nice funny guy any day. She knew this and she tried to fight it, but her cunt wanted what it wanted and she wasn't gonna go all Catholic rosaryhailmaryprayinghairshirtconfessional any time soon; she wasn't gonna privilege the mind over the body. She let her hormones win a lot of the times cos of her own fucked-up doctrine, but at least it was her own.

The professor was saying something about welcome and syllabusing and who he was and that was taking a long time and he seemed to have a British accent, which usually was a turn on for Homegirl, but she had a feeling prof's British accent was an attempt to lure girls like her into the office after hours and there was a convenient couch there or maybe not, maybe he'd expect the girl just to throw herself on top his desk and she'd of course be wearing a garter belt sans panties and she'd spread her legs and spread her butt cheeks with her hands to help him find the right spot cos he was almost doddering, he was like 50 or something. Not really, she knew, 50 wasn't doddering, even tho it seemed so far away.

Homegirl was staring kinda behind the prof cos his mouth was getting spitty as he talked and she was starting to feel sorry for him and she didn't know if she could stay in a class where she felt sorry for the person in charge when she noticed the door opening and that's when he walked in.

He. Oh shit. He. He walks in. She immediately forgets about the prof's spitty mouth cos her cunt's going all kinds of crazy wet almost instantaneously. This guy's tall with brown swept back hair and blue eyes and she wants to stop staring cos she feels like if he catches her staring he will catch her up but she can't and he's wearing a white button down shirt and faded but not too faded jeans that hang but hang just right on his long lean form and she tries to get a glimpse of his shoes cos then she'd really know but there are all these people in her way and she wishes it was just the two of them; she feels like it's just the two of them. The beautiful people, and it feels fated and she should know better and she does know better cos of what happened with her and the ex-Marine when she thought it was fated cos she felt something primal the first time their eyes met and the little spitty prof's saying something sarcastic about punctuality in his spitty fake Brit accent and he, this guy, doesn't seem to care, he just glides past all her classmates and pulls out the chair next to her and actually says, in the middle of class, even, Anyone sitting here?

He's got a deepass voice of course and now she's not feeling like a guy at all but like a woman, like a shy woman, like a swooning woman, like a woman who's blushing and she is blushing, she can feel it and she doesn't trust her voice and so just shakes her head and he sits down next to her and she feels her leg, the one closest to him, pulled towards him and she feels all kinds of tingly and she's wondering if this happens to everyone at some point in their lives, this animal attraction, this magnetism, this moth to light, this junebug to screendoor response. The junebug buzzing buzzing into the screendoor, hitting it and falling to the ground and getting back up all dizzy and hitting it again, wanting in so bad. Her leg keeps moving near him and she has no idea what the prof's saying and she's afraid her leg will brush his and she'll orgasm right there and then and all of a sudden she hears chairs scraping and people are getting up and she's like what the fuck. Did I just come and clear the whole room out?

Cigarette break, he says.

Wanna join me?, he says.

She doesn't smoke unless she's drunk, like I said, but she's feeling über-drunk right now. She nods yes. She still hasn't said anything to him; she doesn't know when she'll find her voice.

SIX

I've given you dive bars and a hill and a café somewheres but I haven't given you any local color; I haven't grounded you in the scene. If you were a realist, you wouldn't believe me. If you were a realist, you'd hate me, even.

If I were a realist, I'd hate me, but for different reasons; I'd be so bored with myself and my realism, I'd go to one of the corner bars in Miltown and drink and drink and drink until I couldn't even remember my name and then everything'd become surreal and it'd be surreal and absurd wherever I ended up – a stranger's bed, a psych ward, the hospital, the gutter, the median, the cop shop, on a bicycle, in space, wherever.

& I am fascinated by medians and I dig people who also obsess about them…

It def wouldn't be realistic cos I would see things I wasn't supposed to see.

Like what the insides of my intestines look like: bright yellow and stringy.

& what your bourgeois dreams look like: bright yellow with stainless steel stringy-ass accessories.

& what the lushes call aurora borealis is really just dawn flashing on dting eyelids.

& what bike sex looks like: ask O'Brien.

& what the normal workday looks like: newspaper print and kitty vomit.

& what life and death means to corporations: Hello, kitty!

& what married couples' sex lives look like: walruses frozen in ice.

& what married couples call love: Bill Cosby sucking jello pudding pops.

& what Punkboy calls love: home.

& what Richboy calls love: cruelty.

& what Homegirl calls love:

& Homegirl will fantasize about walking these streets like a noir antihero fucking every attractive guy/girl she meets and leaving a bloody trail down these Miltown sidewalks.

But, I haven't even described Miltown so you are in an everyplace everywhere howtown.

Upside down, even.

Miltown is a city that wants to be a small town; Miltown can be blue collar and Miltown can be haute couture. Miltown is everything and everyone on a microcosmic macrocosm.

Punkboy and Richboy and Homegirl all live within walking distance of each other, in the somewhat gentrifying artist/student/poor section of the city. The gentrification is pushing the poorer peoples further into the "inner city."

The "inner city" is made up of "others."

Thanks, Edward Said and all you theorists.

Miltown is an extremely racially segregated city and thus, a microcosm of the U.S.

That is my soapbox. I am done now. Let's get back to the sexings.

Where Homegirl and Richboy and Punkboy live, there are many duplexes. They are all at least two stories and there are basements and outside porches without screens and some of the porches seem to be rotting, especially the railings and there's a punk rock coffee shop near them all, but it's not the café that Homegirl and Punkboy work at, tho it's owned by the same people.

The one they work at's located in the more bohemian, less studenty section of town.

Or is it the more rich studenty and less poor artist section of town?

Whatever it is, there's a lot more money involved and a lot of the workers walk or skateboard or bike over the bridge to work there. When Homegirl first started working there she walked cos she didn't own a car; she was poorer than she is now. But not by much.

She used part of her financial aid to pay for her wee car, but don't tell Uncle Sam.

The café Punkboy and Homegirl work at's called Rockit and there are rockets and rabbits all over and it's cheesy and there're big air ducts exposed and the walls are red and they have new "artist exhibits" going up every month and Punkboy's only supposed to play his grindcore at close when the three person crew (four if they're training someone new) gets down and cleans the whole fucking place in like an hour. Push broom and mop and ammonia water and cigarette smoking and beer drinking and till counting and grindcore grindcore and every now and then bootyhouse bootyhouse for the girls and pint glasses washing and pint glasses smashing every now and then and bleach rags wiping wiping and every now and then lines in the one person women or men's bathroom.

The crew tries to do it fast fast fast. Sometimes they have

time to sit and smoke cigarettes and finish their beers before the hour's up.

Homegirl hates the mopping and always wants the mens to do the mopping and then she feels like a bad feminist and then she thinks when have I ever been a true feminist and then she thinks maybe she's subverting the system from within and then she tries to fool herself, like all third wavers, that using your feminine sexual wiles is feminism.

There's no place for feminism in food service; bitches are lucky they're even let in the kitchen.

That ain't my soapbox.

And there's no real place for punk rock at the café but the owners pretend and leave them alone most of the time and the punk rockers gotta survive somehow. And the owners know there's more cultural collateral in the pierced, tattooed freaks than in the strait-laced. Not to mention more scintillation.

Their customers can pretend they're bohemian by having their coffee/breakfast/lunch/even dinner served to them by young punkish freaks.

Homegirl has one tattoo and it's a bad tattoo; Homegirl has more piercings than that and they're all good.

But what does this tell you about Miltown?

Miltown is a city where when Homegirl saw the Ex-Marine and he was wearing the baggy faded rolled-up jeans and the wallet with the chain attached and this was early before everyone in Miltown was doing it and he'd brought it here, probably, cos he'd been a Marine and been around the world and definitely to Saudi Arabia and maybe to Europe, she thought he was so fucking cool cos no one, and I really mean no one and this is not Homegirl's love or infatuation talking, no one had the wallet with chain except him at first.

& Homegirl loved him.

Miltown is a city that can be swept away like that. Just like Homegirl; maybe she's a product of her environment, eh? One cool thing at the right time and the whole city's on fire; one uncool thing at the wrong time and the whole city's on fire, too.

If they closed the bars or taxed them more, there would be a lush riot.

There are bars on almost every corner where Richboy and Homegirl and Punkboy live; it's a lush's Mecca and the lushes hear the call to drink more than twice a day and they bow and they genuflect and scrape knees on pavement and bow heads into walls and sidewalks only as they're leaving the bars.

Richboy and Homegirl are students and Punkboy's food service and Homegirl's food service and a student and they all go to bars.

What I'm trying to say's food service's where it's at. Don't let no one tell you different.

Okay, maybe it's not. Maybe that's my surreal median self talking. But, it's better than office work, I guess.

Yes it is.

SEVEN

So just who is this Homegirl? Why is she this breathing living needing wanting wanting thing?

First grade Homegirl = long stringy hair her mother put in two skinny-ass braids. Her mother should've known better, and yes, Homegirl has a family and yes, she has a mother and father. She didn't spring fully clothed in black, reading Camus and smoking Gauloises, from Nabokov's head as she'd like everyone to think.

She doesn't hang with her fam much, tho, cos they don't get her and they bring her down. Her parents are all like when are you gonna get married and make me some grandchilluns and her sibs are all like look at our babies.

Homegirl grew up in the burbs and had buck teeth until her insolvent parents sent her to a training program for orthodontics where the students made fun of her ropey saliva. Her parents went bankrupt in between her and her sisters' orthodontia. Bad investments or something. Maybe all the Izods and shit they bought for the three eldest girls. The Jaguar for the eldest's graduation. Maybe some coke on her father's part and definitely the drink. It was the eighties after all. Homegirl had a fauxhawk then and wanted to be punk rock. But back to first grade Homegirl.

She had a friend I'll call Futureslut. Futureslut and Homegirl were chased home by older boys for years. Futureslut wanted to be a writer. Furtureslut thought a lot. Futureslut liked the boys to chase and wanted to be caught. Homegirl liked the boys to chase, but didn't want to be caught. The older boys often had things like big squeeze jars of paint they'd stolen from art class and they threatened to paint Futureslut and Homegirl.

Futureslut imagined her body wriggling wriggling in their hands.

Homegirl didn't want her clothes dirtied; Homegirl's always cared about how she's looked, except for seventh grade when her metabolism slowed down and her eating increased and she put on like twenty pounds and then over that summer she grew grew grew and by the time she hit high school she was super skinny. & by the time she hit high school she was determined she'd stay that way.

Even Homegirls are not oblivious to media conditioning, even if they try to fight it.

During recess in first and second grade, the first and second graders played boys chase girls and girls chase boys. There were two large concrete tunnels on the playground, one pink and one blue. When the boys chased the girls, if they caught you, they'd take you to the blue tunnel.

Some girls acquiesced and walked daintily between their captors; Homegirl always fought when she got caught.

She liked the fighting as much as the chase.

She liked all the adrenaline and stuff involved.

If she weren't so young she would have realized the chase and subsequent fight turned her on.

She liked the fighting as much as Futureslut liked the idea of wriggling under big boy hands.

Homegirl was sad when her classmates outgrew the game. She and Futureslut couldn't fight the older boys who chased them cos these boys were in junior high, one was even about to graduate. Plus, Futureslut didn't want to fight; she wanted to acquiesce, which is probably why she was one of the first junior high girls to give it up. I don't even know why I put "girls" there cos no one ever says that about a boy.

He gave it up in junior high.

What a slut; he just gave it up.

Homegirl was a lot older than junior high and Homegirl lost it to a pool shark. She was dating the pool shark; she hadn't lost a bet. Tho one time before Punkboy she'd been playing bar dice at the dive bar and the bartender bet her that she had to show up on his porch and strip and she lost.

She reneged immediately. The bartender'd dated one of the owners of the café she worked at and he had a big head. Homegirl didn't need any of that.

Homegirl decided that summer between seventh and eighth grade when she dropped those extra pounds that she'd become punk rock. She'd become an outcast in the nice suburb she lived in anyway cos her parents'd just bankrupted and that showed that god didn't love them. Plus, physical imperfection was not tolerated cos that meant god didn't love you, too, especially since Homegirl had three older sisters who'd never had an extra pound of fat on them, never a hair out of place on their neatly styled bobs, never a pimple to be seen through their Estee Lauder or Lancome foundation, and never a hint of perspiration to be whiffed through their CK One. Homegirl sweated and ate and ached and sweated more over that summer and came out of it with a fauxhawk and Egyptian kohled eyes. & she kept this up through freshman year and got things thrown at her and then sophomore year she stopped eating and grew her hair out and looked like a ballerina.

It was in that fat transitional period that Homegirl fell in love with Tubesockboy. In high school, Tubesockboy was caught in his backyard trying to even out a farmer's tan by wearing tubesocks on his arms. He became an outcast, kind of, too. Homegirl was in seventh grade and didn't care; she thought he was cu-oote. Plus she was outcast, like I said. Tubesockboy grew up, went to college, married a gorgeous woman who supported him emotionally *and* gave great blowjobs (and a bitch like that's hard to find), and had two beautiful children; Homegirl not so much, not the degree, the spouse who eats her out, the children or any of it, but you probably figured that out already.

Homegirl's thinking she should have taken it farther when she was younger; she shoulda worn tubesocks all over. She shouldn't have cared so much what anyone thought.

She did have a fauxhawk for a while, like I said. It was ghastly.

And she had metal braces.

She never had acne, tho. She was lucky that way. Instead she uglied herself to get through her pre-teen years and then reversed and tried to fit in again. By that time, Tubesockboy was already gone Ivy-leaguing, meeting hottie-wife-to-be, both of them walking back arms full of books from an all-night study session at the library to their apartments pre-dawn and they fall in with each other and the sun's just peeking through and there's an empty construction lot and he says, Want to?, and she nods and there's a crane and neither of them have ever been in a crane, let alone fucked in a crane, and so they have at it and the sun rises through the crane's huge windshield and she's straddling him and welcoming him and the sun and they come and the sun's officially risen and it's love love love.

Tubesockboy was Homegirl's first crush; she shoulda gone out & gotten him. She shouldn't have been so afraid of rejection. But, if she had, there'd be one less crane-sex experience in the world.

Maybe.

She still shouldn't care so much what anyone thinks, but that's my insight, not hers.

Sometimes tho Homegirl dreams of Tubesockboy and he's got those tubesocks on and he looks so small and he's doing some weird stiff-armed robot dance or maybe he's running back and forth or maybe she's the one that's moving and maybe his arms are just outstretched like he's trying to catch something and it's summer and quiet cos the sun hasn't come up quite yet and a bat flies by so close to her head and she's swaying through the air but she hasn't caught on and so she looks around and up and down and then figures out she's the one moving, she's upside down, suspended somehow from a wrecking ball.

EIGHT

Homegirl woke up early; Punkboy was snoring snoring next to her and she just didn't have the patience to keep laying next to him pretending to be sleeping until his tatted fingers started moving all over her, looking for her clit, looking to see if she was wet. Punkboy almost always woke up hard; Homegirl usually liked that about him. She usually went along with the pretend that he was the initiator, the hunter, the predator, that he was the one looking for sex, looking to see if she was ready or, better yet, if he could make her ready.

This morning, tho, she was feeling out of sorts and rolled quietly off her side of the bed. Punkboy snored still and she padded barefoot to her pile of clothing on the floor. Of course, they'd fucked again after coming home from the dive bar. When together she and Punkboy were like two virgin teenagers set loose in a Texas cathouse. Or some other weird simile about sex and virgins and teenagers and Texan whores, but that's the best I can come up with right now.

Homegirl had to work that night, but Punkboy had off. Maybe that was contributing to her offness. She didn't know. She put on her miniskirt and her kneehigh boots and her bra and her shirt and couldn't find her panties, but didn't care. Punkboy'd take care of them; he'd probably clean and hand them back to her all folded nicely the next time they worked together. Surreptitiously, of course, so no one would know.

She didn't know if he just pretended to her that none of the boys knew or if he hadn't told them. She hadn't told the girls yet cos the last time she'd told one of the café bitches about having something with one of their co-workers, some kind of feeling for him, the bitch'd waited until she took her vacation to Montreal and when she'd come back, the two were a couple and in love and making out in the small back room that served as both supply/mop room and employee changing/time card room. She had to push past them to punch in; what she'd really wanted to do was punch the bitch out cold and suck face with dude over, maybe even on, the passed out body.

Those café bitches were always all around stealing your love.

That may be my insight, tho. It's already hard to tell.

She did care that she and Punkboy almost always had different nights off; she was always worried he was meeting up with other girls on those nights; she was always worried he'd fall in love on one of those nights off and come into work the next night with hickeys and rope burns and even a new tattoo.

She'd never inspired that kind of love; she'd never caused a guy to get a new tatt ever.

That she knew. & it probably didn't count if you didn't. In fact, I'd like to say it's hella creepy if you don't. That's like pure stalking territory. Not like I'd know.

She grabbed her purse from the doorknob; she didn't remember leaving it there, but that didn't bother her.

There were a lot of worse things not to remember.

Homegirl left Punkboy's bedroom quietly. Punkboy was almost thirty, but he had a roommate, some big shadowy guy

RYDER COLLINS

who smoked a lot of pot and didn't hang with any scenes. Punkboy's roommate gave Homegirl the creeps. She called him Shadow, except to his face. To his face all she said was, Hi, if she had to. She was always always hoping not to run into him on her naked way to the bathroom after she and Punkboy'd fucked for hours.

She knew he listened to them doing it and jerked off. She knew he thought about her cunt and she knew, somehow, he thought of it as glistening.

That really creeped her out. Anyone who daydreamed about a glistening cunt creeped her out. Cunts don't glisten. They get moist; they get wet; they make inappropriate sucking sounds, they quiver and fasten around cock shafts, they've got fucking minds of their own, but they don't glisten and they don't sparkle unless you're a stripper and douched with glitter. Yeah, there were pretty cunts just like there were pretty cocks. Punkboy liked to look at her cunt a lot, so hers must have been a-ight. His cock was nicey-nice to look at, too. He'd sent her a jpeg of it via his cell phone. She'd look at it when she was having a bad day, when Richboy didn't call, when her two roommates, both guys cos there was no way in hell Homegirl was gonna put up with bitch roommates macking on her mens, were pissing her off, or when she had to work counter at the café.

She hated working counter; she hated being fake nice and usually couldn't be bothered. Usually she said, Can I help you? & then rang up the order & then said, (whatever the total was), please. All without smiling or inflection.

There'd been a really cute boy that'd starting coming

37

in every night at the café; she and her friends called him Prettyboy. The second week she'd waited on Prettyboy she'd knocked over his pint of coffee on the counter, which was conveniently crotch level on a lot of guys.

She said, I'm so sorry.

She said, Here's my rag. And tossed him a damp towel to wipe himself down with. At least she knew better than to wipe his crotch down herself. That would have been pure Hollywood bullshit and would've freaked Prettyboy out even more.

He was already freaked out; she could tell.

The next night he didn't even say hi when he ordered his pint and he wouldn't look her in the eye. She'd decided there went her chances with Prettyboy, which was probably okay, in hindsight, cos who wants to date a guy who's prettier than them?

That crotch fiasco was only one of the reasons she liked to work kitchen instead. She never had to worry about what people thought about her when she cooked. She could talk the dirty talks or not talk at all. She could be hungover and run to the bathroom and vomit and then come right back and continue making sandwiches like the professional she wanted to be.

Secretly she wasn't a professional cos her Catholic mother'd instilled in her one mother of a superego. That bitch was always and forever trying to repress her impulses. It's why she wanted to be a professional but couldn't; it was one fuck of a never-ending cycle.

Homegirl even felt a little guilty about being creeped out

by Shadow. She'd made it to the stairs this morning without seeing him. Shadow and Punkboy rented an entire house instead of a flat like most of the people she knew, herself included; it was a small house, but still, Homegirl kinda wondered how they could afford it.

But she only kinda wondered. She didn't want to know that much about Shadow.

She was at the bottom of the stairs and then there was Shadow. He was going to walk past her going up it looked like. He was gonna squeeze past her and "accidentally" brush her side, her hip, her breast, some of the places she knew he wanted to molest. He was a big bald guy with neck rolls and as he approached her he seemed to make himself bigger.

Hey, he said as he brushed past her. She smelled onion stank breath; she tried to make herself smaller but she was a tall hippy Midwest thing.

She wanted to say, Hey, you fuck. I know what you're doing.

She wanted to say, You're such a fucking Chester.

She wanted to say, Touch me again and I'll cut your nuts off in your sleep.

What she said was, Hey, cos he scared her more than she wanted to let on, scared her way more than the boys she loved to fuck and if she said anything he would know he scared her and he'd have some kind of power over her and above all Homegirl never wanted anyone she didn't love to have power over her cos she was forever and always letting those she loved or thought she loved or even sometimes those she really really liked to fuck have power over her and that was more than

39

fucking enough. Then she shot the fuck out of there like that loose cannon she wanted to be.

NINE

For their "first date," Richboy and Homegirl met up at a dive bar. I gots the ironic quotes around first date cos they'd already seen each other naked, they'd gone home together after the first workshop the prof held in the bar, so that kind of first-date anxiety – are we gonna click, are we gonna do it, should I whack off first so I'm thinking with my head and not my dick/pussy? – was tot missing from this date.

It was a different dive bar than the dive bar Punkboy and Homegirl liked to hang at. This dive bar'd just been repainted white while the other hadn't been re-painted white in years. This dive bar was a big coke bar. So was the other dive bar, but Punkboy didn't do coke and Richboy did whatever he could get his big rich hands on.

His hands were big and always grabbing grabbing. He liked to think of himself as a Darwinian. He liked to think of himself as in Rousseau's state of nature. He liked to think of himself as avant-garde. He didn't like to think of himself as what he was: an apathetic narcissist with a trust fund. Homegirl sometimes saw him as her Noble Savage and she didn't want to bring civilization to that; she wanted him to sweep her up into his arms and they would get lost in that state of nature forever and ever.

Homegirl was a Romantic but she would never admit it; she wanted everyone to think she was tough, beyond emotions. She slept around to prove this. She fucks cos she can and she

41

don't let em know how much the fucking means to her. She still hadn't learned the tubesocks lesson. Own your weird shit, Homegirl, own it.

It's all you can do in this life. So fucking own it.

Richboy didn't own his weird shit cos Richboy wasn't really weird; he was bored and affected and thought acting weird was cool.

He woulda been a jock boy if he had any athletic propensities; it was the book learnings that led him down this tortured aesthete path.

He'd strewn the path with the hearts of girls and boys he'd encountered. He was always always on the lookout for a tortured artist heart, tho.

That was the prize.

He thought maybe they could change him, those artists with the big tortured hearts; they could make him feel something for reals. He knew downdeep he was a cliché and this knowledge was what caused him to drink and piss himself and go drugging and snorting and smoking and pilling and coking and tripping through life. There was a voice in his head that was always always commenting; there was a voice in his head that sounded like Baudrillard; there was a voice in his head with a French accent and a craving for Nutella and big milky cups of coffee; there was a voice in his head that sometimes wore an ironic beret and propelled him to McDonald's; there was a voice in his head that told him he was inauthentic – that everything he did and said and thought'd been constructed for him by someone else and he'd never ever escape this and it was his burden and maybe if he'd been born poor he could drink tallboys of Pibber gladly and if he'd been born poor he could read Bukowski freely and if he'd been born someone else he could be happy.

He wanted to be someone else and it filled him with a self-loathing that made him only think about himself and how he wanted to be someone else.

But, this was supposed to be all about the lovebirds' first date at the dive bar that is not Punkboy's dive bar.

I'd put lovebirds in quotes, too, but you might find that disingenuous or at the very least, inauthentic.

A simulacrum or some shit.

Richboy was already at the bar drinking a tallboy of Pibber when Homegirl showed up. She was a few minutes late, not cos she wanted to be cool or so Richboy wouldn't think she was too eager but cos she'd been hit by a wave of anxiety she'd needed three swigs from her emergency bottle of Maker's to overcome. Even tho she'd already seen Richboy naked and liked it, she was still anxious about whether or not he liked her.

The anxiety was not first date anxiety, tho; this anxiety was deeper and dirtier.

She'd smothered this anxiety in black eyeliner and smokey eyes, in red red lipstick and pale skin, in a short short skirt and tall boots; she smothered it in thoughts of smoking Richboy's cigarettes, which will always always throughout the centuries even after fags are outlawed be a metaphor.

You know.

Hey, she said and slid into the barstool next to his.

What's. Up, he said. He said it like that. Exactly.

She smiled and looked down and didn't know why.

& Richboy thought, Oh yes. I gots this one.

& he did have her cos Homegirl thought and thought about him and what she thought was how he could make her always strong. She would always have to be strong around him; she could never show her weaknesses, those stupid things she did, the hair on her toes, those things she hated about herself. Just being around him would keep her vigilant, striving. She would be the strongest and coolest motherfucking homegirl she ever knew, if only he never caught on to how she really was inside.

That part of her inside would go away with his love, she hoped.

Richboy said, What're you having?

A Guinness, she said, and then thought she should've gotten a Pibber like him. She would have to be more vigilant. She couldn't let him know that she'd changed her mind, tho.

He waved the bartender over and got her a beer and she smiled and looked down again and felt things moving underneath the smothering, underneath the anxiety even. There were things moving and she felt them moving and she wanted to protect these moving feeling things. She wanted to be careful.

Instead she asked Richboy for a smoke even before she got her beer.

He handed her a Camel and she put it in her mouth and then had to bend for a light, like she knew she would.

She took this as a sign.

The bartender put her beer down and took a couple of bills

from the pile in front of Richboy.

Thanks, she said and looked at him. He was brushing his hair back from his face; he looked serious; he looked like he was thinking somethings.

My pleasure, he said. Have you ever read Genet?

Homegirl didn't want to say no cos she didn't want to seem uncool but it'd be even uncooler, she knew, if he found out she was lying cos then it would seem like she wanted to impress him.

And of course she did.

And when her first story was workshopped, his comments were the only ones she'd cared about. Of course. When Homegirl likes a boy it is all thinking about him and thinking about him; it is like that favorite song you have and you play it over and over and over and it moves you and you want to dance or smash or cry or get high.

Richboy is Homegirl's favorite song.

What Homegirl always and always forgets is that in a year or a month or sometimes even a week, there'll be a new song. What she always doesn't remember is she'll listen to that one fave song some years later and be all what was so special about this or what was I thinking or this is goddamned embarrassing. Like when she loved loved Duran Duran.

Sometimes the music comes back, but by then it's retro. Homegirl's never had a retroboyfriend.

Although if the ex-Marine came back she'd retro him right in; she'd let him retro her all night and day and night and maybe this time he'd stay. Cos she's so retroactive.

I'll stop now.

45

Homegirl stabbed her smoke out and shook her head.

Richboy started talking about Genet's life and his genius and how he was invited to all these fancy dinner parties after Renoir the director or was it Truffaut? discovered and championed him and how Genet was at this one party and everyone was eating and talking serious pontificating things, deep pensive art talks, and Genet got up and pulled the dinnercloth out from under them.

Ha, Richboy then said.

Ha ha, Homegirl said. She wanted to say more things. Things like, Yeah, fuck the bourgeoisie. Or things like, I will do that some day when I'm a writer. Or, I will be your tablecloth please. But she didn't want Richboy to think she was a dork. & she didn't think she could let him know she was a dork downdeep.

That was part of the insides she didn't like so much.

The bartender came by and Homegirl switched to PBR.

I was at this party in New Orleans once, Richboy said.

Homegirl said, You lived in New Orleans?

Yes, Richboy said.

How was it? I've never been. I lived in London briefly, Homegirl said.

Loved New Orleans. So many parties, such a city of eating breathing loving creating destroying peoples. & I was at this one party and Fred Schneider was there and he was all coked up. You know Fred, right? From the B-52s?, Richboy said.

Yeah, Homegirl said and she wasn't lying. She'd gone through a B-52 New Wave phase after Duran squared.

So Fred was all coked up and he just started pissing in

the corner of this guy's bedroom. Just pissing and singing something, Richboy said.

Was it "Rock Lobster"?, Homegirl said.

I think it was "Planet Claire," Richboy said. Then he pulled two cigarettes from his pack and gave one to Homegirl without her even asking.

She took that as a sign, too.

TEN

Look, I know you and I aren't on the same wavelength. You watch *America's Got Talent* or some shit, you've never worked food service, you tip like a cheap bastard because of it, and you've never been properly laid. Ever. No matter how hard you wished.

& by *you*, I don't mean you, of course. I mean that imaginary you out there somewhere, that you, that you that just doesn't get it, that's never been properly fucked or even drunk wrestled.

Cos that you, not *you* but that one you out there somewhere who shops at Trader Joe's unironically and enjoys the clanging bell they ring and even knows why they ring that fucking bell, *that* you's never tried to get laid properly. That would make you a perv. Especially if you tell your husband/wife/nanny/officeboy/babysitter/crossing guard that the old-fashioned deep sea diver's suit is what does it for ya.

You know. The one with the round helmet that screws on. It's like Frankenstein undersea.

Homegirl feels like Frankenstein sometimes and sometimes Homegirl's felt like she was fucking Frankenstein. That's why she's narrowed it down to two guys who don't remind her of re-animated corpses – Punkboy and Richboy.

But this was all about you.

Have you ever had a Punkboy? Have you ever had a Richboy? Ya ha deedle deedle... Homegirl doesn't care about

48

money and Homegirl doesn't care about hygiene so much. I know you do. I know you spent the last hour cleaning your bathroom, collecting the hairs from the bathtub drain, scrubbing the soap from the sink, wiping the piss and blood and cum from around the toilet bowl all the while pretending it doesn't exist.

& that's why I worry about you.

& that's why you'll never be a part of Homegirl's world.

Not until she realizes how much the body can let you down.

Just wait; I know you know.

ELEVEN

Walk of shame; walk of bloody shame. Homegirl didn't know where her panties'd gone, and this time she cared. She was wearing octagonal sunglasses with pinkened lenses, tho, and that helped a little, made her feel untouchable, beyond. She had cottonmouth. She was beyond cottonmouth; she was cottonmouth.

This'd been her sixth time with Richboy and she didn't exactly remember all the details.

She knows he didn't tie her up and let some butch fist her for hours, like she was afraid.

She was almost always afraid of what he'd do and extremely turned on.

The fifth time, when they really didn't have sex, was when she realized she was almost always afraid of him and completely and tot turned on.

Where the hell was her car?

They'd done it for hours last night, she could tell, cos it hurt to walk and that'd only happened a couple of times. Once with Punkboy after they hadn't done it for almost a year and every time with the ex-Marine.

But, Homegirl didn't like to think about the ex-Marine.

So, I'll tell you all about him while Homegirl's looking for her car.

Her panties are in her pocket, by the way. Richboy doesn't need souvenirs; he's got a small surveillance camera set up above his bed that connects with his Mac. He can re-live every moment that he or she forgets.

Richboy doesn't forget that much, tho; he often only pretends he's fucked up. He's got a huge motherfucking tolerance. Boy can drink a fifth of vodka a night; boy drinks only to get fucked up. Richboy doesn't even like the taste of alcohol, that's how bad it is.

Homegirl sometimes likes it and sometimes pretends.

But, back to the ex-Marine... he was the second person ever Homegirl slept with. She loved the sex so much she thought she loved him. She thought she loved him so much she wanted him to stay with her always and always; she wanted to give him things; she wanted him to give her things. Any things. Nylons, candy, Japanese fans; she didn't care if he were channeling a WWI or II Marine. Lipstick, hula hoops, riding boots, embossed stationery, handkerchiefs, straight razor, rug burn, anything would do. Tangible proof that there was something there. Tangible proof that he existed. Tangible proof that he'd touched her. Tangible proof that he'd touched her there. Even an STD would do.

Proof he'd been there; proof she could remember forever. She'd wanted him to give her warts cos it wasn't as bad as Herpes but still left scars; she'd still love him; she'd even try to fuck him after a wart-freezing treatment cos he showed up at her house with glitter on him and wanted to fuck.

The glitter was from Art's Performing Center, a downtown strip joint.

Homegirl'd kinda knew he was seeing other people, but he fucked oh so good, she couldn't leave him, especially now that she had proof. Now that he'd marked her as his territory; now that his virus'd explored and cartographed and made her his.

It'd hurt so bad for Homegirl because of the coochie freezing that ex-Marine'd be able to tell and he'd stop and say, Let's just cuddle. Cos, deep down he's always been a hooker with a heart of gold.

At least that's what Homegirl's always wanted to think, then, now and foreverever.

He is her heart of gold she's been looking for and he's gone.

She will keep on looking for that feeling that fucking him'd always given.

She'll keep on looking for his heart of gold in all the other mens she meets.

She'd never really wanted him to give her an STD, tho. That was her hyperbole, her melodrama, the part of her that imagines herself in a film noir with seamed stockings and a big hat and even bigger hips and a cigarette holder in an alley with ex-Marine or Richboy or whoever and it's raining but her hat protects her cigarette and her lips are oh so red but oh so black cos it's all in black and white and words are said and it doesn't matter what words are said, the words are said they can't be unsaid but they aren't words you'd wish unsaid anyway cos this is noir fantasy and those words that should never be said and can't be unsaid only and forever exist in reality; the rain and the smoke and the alley and the pouting lips are enough forever, they are more than words, said or wished unsaid.

She did wish the ex-Marine'd stay with her foreverever, but life's one fuck of a bitch who'll show you what you want then laugh and say, Never gonna get it.

Like that fucking En Vogue song, and that's just so wrong on so many levels.

Life's a bitch that laughs at you as you stare into the window of some chi-chi department store and you're a street urchin and you're Oliver fucking Twist and the bad men are gonna make you steal just to stay alive but what you really want is an evening dress and the appropriate soirée to wear it to but life's bored, life's got bad ennui and kicking a girl when she's down is the best possible solution.

Life watches *America's Funniest Home Videos* in its tidy whities and clubs the dog with a baseball bat for no reason really.

Homegirl likes Richboy cos he's a lot like life.

Homegirl likes Richboy cos she thinks she sees something in him like the ex-Marine.

Something choking down deep that the tongue can unlick from hiding.

There are things in him that say, I will show you things you've never seen.

Homegirl thinks he knows things. That he's one of those people who are living those lives. The lives that we don't know about. The lives where things happen. Where things become and things show and things are unraveled and things are reconstructed and things are more than things. She thinks if she hangs on long enough he will let her see these things, too. She hopes if she can intrigue him long enough he will look for things like love in her; that the love things will naturally lead him to showing her the things she knows he wants to show someone. The love things will be their things; her thing will be to keep him safe and be a place for him to put his hand when he wants to feel some thing and she'll wipe his oily hair from his brow when he's drunk and she'll caress his head always and forever and it will feel like love this wiping, caressing and being wet thing, and his thing will be to show her the things he knows she would never know, and the showing of these things will also feel like love.

The things like love are what happens between the burlesque dancer, the S&M mistress, and the pierced guy who hangs from hooks after the performances are over and the club closes. The things like love is how bored you have to be to watch scheisse videos or how many kilos of coke it takes to convince a girl to shit on a glass table in front of you. Or how to make people like you without even trying and how to push them away but still keep them coming back. Or how to tap into that mammalian pack mentality and rule people instinctually. Or how many people sleep naked and how many people sleep fully clothed afraid of something entering their orifices in the night. The things like love are how many people at any given time are reading Genet and masturbating vs. how many Acker. What money really means and why privileged white boys are so angsty.

The things like love are also stupid things like how to act like you don't care which knife or fork you should use at dinner. Or how not to care when salad leaves don't behave and stick out your mouth. Or what to say at a family dinner when politics come up and you just don't fucking care or you care too much.

The things like love are also body things. Not just sex; not just the genital slamming genital thing and the ooohing and the sighing and the scrunched up orgasm face thing, but body things like how to get rid of bad breath or how to never have it in the first place. How to brush one's tongue without gagging. How to drink and drink and drink and drink without gaining weight.

Homegirl'd really liked to know the secret of that one.

The ex-Marine probably knew things, too, but the ex-Marine'd thought love things meant protecting his love from those knowing things.

Homegirl wants to be protected and live a nicey-nice life, and Homegirl doesn't. Homegirl doesn't really know what she wants besides someone to wake up to when she wants to and someone who knows when to let her sleep it off alone.

Richboy seems to get it; he seems to get her.

That may be her love things talking, tho.

Homegirl's intuition wasn't always right and sometimes she ignored her intuition and she thought Richboy probably always listened to his and she looked up to him, kinda and that's the kinda shit that'd make him ballistic, if he knew.

If he knew she looked up to him, for reals, he'd make sure she never did again.

TWELVE

For Richboy, love is a beating thing; love is a frog. Love is a tadpole you scoop out of pond scum and hold wiggling in your palm and you hold it there and watch it squirm and it squirms its small moist life against you and you feel something and you can let that thing grow and it will grow into a frog and it will have those long strong back legs and it will jumpkick its ass out of your hand at its first chance, you know, but you hope against hope the frog will stay there contented in your hand or you can start to feel something in the small moist thing and you know what comes next, what the frog'll do cos it's happened before and you can't take this feeling, beating, kicking, wettish thing so you close your hand quickly and squish the little squirmer before it can even get its fucking legs.

For Punkboy, love is a cat that creeps up slowly on soft padded paws and you don't hear or see or smell or even feel this creeping stalking thing and then it's there in your lap and it's purring and rubbing and biting and clawing and catnippy and then it's jumping free and chasing and being chased and catnippy again and there is the wailing and the barbed penis and the being stuck together and it's scary and crazy and you're afraid of the pulling out and you are oh so high.

We know what it is for Homegirl; or what Homegirl thinks it is.

THIRTEEN

Richboy kissed Homegirl's bare shoulder and pulled her closer under the sheets.

They were in Richboy's room, on Richboy's king sized bed that took up most of the room. Richboy was lucky cos he lived alone and used the spare bedroom as his writing office. All he had in his bedroom was his bed and a broken dresser and condoms underneath his pillow. Most of the condoms Homegirl'd brought over and dumped out of her purse when she was drunk the six times before.

Richboy didn't count the times, tho. He didn't need to. He knew the babes would hang on as long as they could hang on; he knew he'd get bored sooner or later.

Sometimes he hoped for later; sometimes he hoped for sooner.

He wasn't hoping for anything with Homegirl; he was just being for once. Maybe cos she was a lot like him and not like him at all. Maybe cos she got him and didn't get him. Maybe cos she got the surprising deepdown things about him and didn't get the surface ones at all; maybe cos she knew why he was the way he was but didn't believe he was really the way he was. Or maybe cos she had a nice little twat. Or maybe cos he liked her.

Maybe not.

He was enjoying this being thing. This just being thing.

He pulled her closer and squeezed her. He said, Baby.

He said, Baby. My. Baby.

& he shouldn't have done that. & he shouldn't have tried to get any closer. & he knew this & he would always look back at this as the moment when he knew he shouldn't have tried, when he knew he was pushing it or whatever.

The world was always always out to get him cos that was the way the world worked & if you hadn't realized that yet, that the world was out to get you, too, then you were an idiot or a chump or realreal motherfucking lucky.

Cos as soon as he pulled her closer she said, We need to talk.

Richboy said, What about, baby?

Richboy was pretending like he didn't care or something. Like he didn't know something was going down. Like maybe it would go away.

But he knew it was something bad and he knew it was gonna explode this just being feeling all in his face. Like a fucked up money shot gone backwards somehow it was gonna cream all over his own eyeballs and in his ears. She was gonna ruin it and she was gonna ruin it even more by doing something cliché like running her bony fingers through his chest hair while she was ruining it. Something clichéd like stopping the chest hair caressing and pulling to slap his chest when she really got going in the ruining of the just being feeling. There was nothing worse than ruining that feeling than adding cliché to really fuck up that feeling, to make sure that feeling knows it's fucked, that that feeling has had its ass handed to it, that that feeling's on its way to the ICU and will soon die alone. Ungrieved.

But, like I said, all he said was, What about, baby?

She said, Oh, Richboy. & she started crying.

Great, Richboy thought, no chest hair caresses at all, straight to the sobbing. How fucking cliché and banal. Maybe I should try to fuck her right now, he thought. Maybe that'll shut her up. He started to move his hand down to her cunt.

She turned over on her side, away from him, and cried some more.

He put his arms around her like he cared. At this point he didn't; he just wanted her to stop pissing on the grave of that feeling. Tell me, he said.

Homegirl turned back to him.

I'm pregnant, she said.

He reached his hand down to her cunt; he would fuck her to make her shut up. He would fuck her and maybe that just being feeling would come back for a little while. Maybe he could play footsies with that being feeling; maybe if he fucked and pretended and fucked and pretended some more the fetus would go away and the being feeling would come back.

He didn't want anything to intrude on his just being feeling.

Anything.

For reals.

FOURTEEN

Casualty had three moods – stoned, more stoned, and comatose. When you heard Clutch blasting from the house at ten a.m., you knew he was well on his way to the third.

& yes, Homegirl heard Clutch as she approached her front door. Fuck, she was hoping for a more lucid Casualty. She'd just been followed by a creeper the entire walk home.

Homegirl lived with two guys - Casualty and Artfag. Casualty was a casualty; he'd already done too many drugs in his short life. He worked at the café with Homegirl when he needed to add more autonomy than his partnership with his dad selling dank dank buds brought in and that's how they'd met; he'd been living with his dad in a big rundown house/grow operation. Artfag had dubbed himself Artfag years ago in a hipster ironic way; he wore big glasses and small jeans and vintage tees and went to art school and answered Homegirl and Casualty's ad for a roommate and was never home but when he was made Homegirl feel a little awkward, even uncool cos he was hipster beyond her years. She usually didn't say much to Artfag when he wasn't out banging some twee girl or guy or at some cool underground arty happening that Homegirl'd only peripherally heard about (and that just proved to her there were all these people out there doing interesting things, people connected to the pulse of life) cos she felt like he was always judging judging every word she said cos she just wasn't too good at irony; she tried too hard and that was the rub. She cared too damn much, tho she tried to pretend she didn't, which made it even worse sometimes cos the pretending was trying and hipsters don't try they just be and yawn.

Homegirl said, Hi. She sat down on the orange nubby couch next to Casualty.

Casualty asked, Ole Faithful?

Ole Faithful was his three foot bong and a reference to punctual gangas eruptions, of course.

Homegirl shook her head and almost started crying. She kinda didn't know why, so she punched Casualty in the arm.

Casualty said, What?

Then, Not cool.

Then, Space cake?

Casualty often lost the ability to form complete sentences and thoughts, but he was cute and sweet and always had those dankass buds. He kept a spice jar of them hidden in plain sight on the café spice rack for emergency situations for all his fellow workers.

& it was much appreciated. Tot appreesh.

Homegirl punched his arm again; this time not as hard.

She said, I was almost raped on the way here.

Then, Hafta work tonight.

Then, Yeah, fuck, give me one.

I think I'm preggers and don't know who the baby daddy is, is what she walked home to say but couldn't. She didn't know why she'd told Richboy about the fetus and not Punkboy. She didn't know why she thought it was Richboy's. She'd walked over after leaving Richboy's house early, without waking him up. She'd walked over after she told him the night before and then they'd fucked and he'd said they'd go for dinner soon and talk and she'd fallen asleep in his arms. She'd walked over cos she needed to think. She'd walked over cos she wanted to be like one of those down on their luck misogynistic outsider guys who are secretly in love but pretend they don't give a fuck. They walk and walk and fuck and walk all over cities; they fuck and walk and there's always some woman they're not in love with they fuck and they don't fuck the woman they deepdown love but still they break her heart, and they walk and walk and walk and leave nothing behind but more broken hearts and cigarette butts.

Homegirl only smoked when she was really really drunk.

Homegirl felt like she'd never have enough something – hutzpah? balls? hatred? entitlement? – to be like one of those young men who could pretend not to love. She wanted to love so bad she scared it away. She'd lie in wait like someone trying to smash a bug or catch an escaped pet – a bird or a rabbit or a gerbil, even; she'd coo and call and hold her hand out gently and when love came she'd try to snatch it, but love was quick and love was always in control. The bird would fly; the rabbit run; the gerbil bitch of love would jump into her palm and then bite til she tried to fling it off, but it would grab on and hold and hang from her fingertip, still biting biting. Love acted upon her. She too often felt acted upon, like she was just reacting to everything and everyone else always around her and never really doing anything of her own volition, never striking out against the forces around her. Always pretending to be a loner, but always and forever still listening to everyone around her and still needing to talk.

She had no one to talk to about the fetus except Casualty; she could trust him not to tell anyone cos he wouldn't remember. She couldn't trust anything he said, though, if he was already on his way to comatose.

He came back with the cake.

Homegirl took a bite.

Fuck, she said.

Fuck, he said.

She knew she shouldn't eat it, but this was her way of fighting. This was her way of saying, I can walk these mean streets even sitting down. I can crush hearts and cigarettes under my well-worn heels; love, I can tip my fedora to you and screw you over without blinking.

It was her way of saying, Fuck you, love.

FIFTEEN

Homegirl texted Richboy, We gots 2 talk now. Can't wait.

Richboy didn't text back; Homegirl waited. Homegirl read a story from workshop. Homegirl went to the bathroom. Homegirl washed her hands and looked at her face. She pulled her bangs away from her forehead to see what she'd look like bangless. She got her flat iron out and waited for it to warm up. She thought she heard the little text jingle-signal and went back to her room.

She passed Casualty in the living room. He asked her if she wanted to partake of Ole Faithful. He seemed to have forgotten this morning already and the space cakes and that Homegirl had to work tonight and that she'd wanted to tell him something. Of course, he'd forgotten.

Homegirl said, No, thanks.

She heard keys in the lock; Artfag was home. She hurried to her room so she wouldn't have to see him and feel inferior.

She checked her phone. No message. Shit. She could wait in here and avoid Artfag or she could go fix her bangs. Then she was like, Why the hell am I hiding out in my own house?

She took her phone with her this time.

Artfag and Casualty were doing bongs on the couch. She waved at Artfag as she walked by. He lifted the bong in greeting.

The bathroom was right off the living room. Some kind of fucked up design. Everyone could hear everything, both ways. Sometimes she'd run the water when she had to shit. She was most shy around Artfag. He was so skinny in his skinny jeans she wondered if he ever ate or shat anymore.

She could hear what passed as convo between Casualty and Artfag as she flattened her bangs obsessively. Her bangs were almost straight to begin with, but she liked those motherfuckers straight. She liked to imagine she'd be at some bar and there'd be a contest and the woman with the straightest bangs would win and she'd rule the bar for a night and every bar denizen would have to carry out her decrees, like every time a Tom Waits song came on everyone would do a shot of bourbon and every time someone said fuck they would have to come kiss the hem of her short skirt or if there were a bunch of creepers there, they'd have to give her a cigarette.

The contest would be decided by a straight ruler. It would be between her and Karen Elson.

Why the fuck not?

Homegirl would win just cos.

Homegirl would win cos she straightens her bangs like a motherfucker, like I said.

& like I said, she could hear Casualty and Artfag.

Casualty was saying, Yeah dude?

Artfag said, Yeah, like I said.

Casualty said, What did ya say again?

Artfag said, I saw him.

Casualty said, Who?

Artfag said, Her boy.

Casualty said, Whose?

Casualty said, Let me see Faithful.

There was the bubbling and the billowing and the suckling of the bongage.

Artfag said, Hers. Homegirl's. Artfag'd seemed to get quieter; Homegirl put the flat iron down and tried to concentrate on what her roommates were saying.

Yeah?, Casualty said.

There were more bong sounds.

Artfag said, Oh man. Yeah.

There was a long exhalation.

What was I saying?, Artfag said.

Something about our girl, Casualty said.

Then there was more flicking, more bubbling, more inhalings and exhalings.

Yeah man, Artfag said. He was with this chick and she had these nice big tits so I went up to talk to her cos papas cannot resist the skinny chicks with the big big tits. You know?

Casualty said, I likes them all.

Casualty was tot being honest and Casualty hadn't been laid in a long time; tho there were a lot of women after him cos he was sweet and handsome and had a buzzed head and blue blue eyes and talked softly and acted interested in everything everyone said, Casualty always always seemed to pass out before any moves could be made on either side. Usually before the girls could make the moves cos by the time he was alone in any kind of room with a girl he was near comatose and didn't have the energy or brains or even the bone marrow to hit on a hot chick. He was jelly and would collapse into whatever cushion was near. Sometimes it was the girl's hip, but it was so non-sexual, she'd either be affronted and leave, letting his head fall wherever, or she'd be comforted and caress his buzzed head and then fall asleep sitting up with a little Casualty on her hip.

The girls that got out were smarter, probably.

Artfag said, I'm picky. This chick was hot, tho. So I went up to her to try to work my magic cos most of them fall for my magic and guess what she says?

Casualty mumbled something Homegirl couldn't hear. Maybe, I'm gay?

Artfag said, No. She said, I'm not interested. So I asked her if I could buy her a drink anyway as a peace token or something and she was like, no, hell no. No money can get in between Richboy and me. We have a deal. It's the only one I'm allowed before Samhain or Satan or Santa Claus or something, I don't know what she said then. Something about how he owns her or something until then. But the rest's for reals, that's what she said. What the hell does that mean?

Casualty was nearing comatose and could only mumble something neither Artfag or Homegirl could make out.

Maybe he'd entered smoker soliloquy stage cos Artfag kept on going, I don't even know why I'm bringing this up. I mean, I've met weird before. I hang with all sorts. I've done flash mobs and other performance arts. But, this was different. Weird in like a creepy eerie knobby tree outside your bedroom window when you're four years old and your parents have left you alone in the house cos they're swinging at the key party down the block kind of way. You know?

Casualty said, Hmmmph, or something like that.

Artfag said, True dat, true dat.

Then he said, I'm on a boat.

Then he said, She was fucking hot, tho.

Casualty said, I'm on a boat.

Another reason Casualty never got laid was that his timing would be always and forever off from all the dankdank buds he smoked. It would always and forever be off until he found that dreadlocked white girl whose sweat smelled like ganga and whose pee smelled like ganga and whose cooch smelled like ganga and they would get married and maybe even have little gangasmelling babies whose timing would be so off it would be on and the babies would grow up to be republicans.

Artfag said, Hot, yeah, big big titties.

Casualty said, I'm on a motherfucking boat.

That's when Richboy texted her, We still on 4 dinner 2morrow?

Homegirl didn't text him back until after she was at work, Yeah. I'll pick you up. Homegirl wanted some semblance of control.

SIXTEEN

These are the things Homegirl remembers from that night; these are not the only things that happened and some of them may not have even happened cos Homegirl's been so drunk she's hallucinated from the drink like Toulouse-motherfucking-Lautrec at least twice before that night, so it's possible some of it's all made up.

It's possible but I know it's not made up.

It was supposed to be a special night, so you know Homegirl shoulda known shit wasn't gonna go down right or that the shit was really gonna go down. I mean, Homegirl's cried consecutively on all her birthdays, her 1st through her 26th, except her 24th.

She got laid that night; she doesn't usually get laid on her bday.

The anticipation, the build-up might have led to all this. Or the fact that Richboy is one sick fuck. But, Homegirl's still kinda in denial on that one. At least until she sees the damage done.

She went to his apartment to pick him up. There was a chick there, in his kitchen, with a big glass of wine and pinot noired lips. Homegirl immediately bristled and immediately tried to hide her reaction; both Richboy and this new chick saw it, tho.

The chick was really thin with straight hips and big big titties; Homegirl was jealous. Homegirl's tits were more than nice but she was curvy like a real woman and not anorexic or boylike, and Homegirl'd been picking up vibes from Richboy lately about her form. Plus, just who the hell was this chick and what was she doing in Richboy's place?

Homegirl, Richboy said, meet Roomy.

They shook hands.

She's my new roommate, Richboy said.

Homegirl wanted to say, Did your trust fund dry up?

Homegirl wanted to say, Where's the bitch sleeping? But, she said nothing. She was always and always like that around the men she really liked. Anyone else she'd tell to fuck off or wouldn't give the time of day to; she could ignore a motherfucker so hard it hurt like you got kicked in the nuts. But, if she really really liked someone she'd be all passive and sincere.

It could be a complete turn-off.

I had to give up my office, Richboy said.

These things are the things Homegirl really remembers cos she only had a swig of Jameson from the bottle before she went to pick Richboy up. She knew better but she'd gotten nervous picking out the right dress. Everything'd looked so gaudy and tight.

Richboy handed her a tallboy of Hamm's. I'm trying to get the hipsters to drink this instead of Pabst, he said.

Homegirl should have taken that crap as a sign and left then. Instead, she popped the can open and chugged to show her skills. Roomy took a petite sip of pinot; Richboy opened himself another Hamm's. It was already his fourth tallboy, but Homegirl didn't know that.

How do you know Richboy? Homegirl asked Roomy.

Craig's list.

Really?

Yeah, she said. There was an ad for a roommate who drinks and reads. That's all it said and I was intrigued.

Really? Homegirl looked at Richboy.

Yeah. Richboy rubbed his hairy chest. He was wearing his shirt unbuttoned low like he wanted to be a 70s pornstar and/or Nick Cave.

This convo Homegirl remembers, this and dinner where she ate awkwardly around Richboy and he insinuated something about her curves she thinks and she ended up paying cos it was in celebration of his story getting published, a story in which a character not unlike her has a small part where she masturbates with a blue umbrella under a park bench and all Homegirl could think when she read it was oooh spiny or oooh expandable; he hadn't described the umbrella so she imagined both an old-fashioned pointy one and a boxy collapsible one, whichever it was way too public and possibly too painful for her masturbatings.

Homegirl has always and forever wished there was a female equivalent to the term *whacking off*. She's used *whacked off* in texts to Punkboy, cos she can tell him anything, but it always and always makes her feel kind of butch.

She likes to be the woman, even with other women.

But, like I said, these are the things she remembers.

& she remembers a lame writing workshop party where there was talk of tazing old ladies and there was talk of zombie literature. She and Richboy got the hell out of there quick.

71

But not before he stopped her in the art deco looking almost *The Shining* apartment hallway and said, I'm a lone wolf.

She imagined twins on trikes knocking into his shins again and again. Maybe she wanted to be one of them or maybe this memory is flavored by what's to come.

They went to a bar and they talked and Richboy said he should call his new roommate cos she didn't know anyone in Miltown and Homegirl said fine but really she didn't want him to so when he didn't she was happy that she had him all to herself among the drunks at the bar.

They went back to his place and Roomy was still up, still sipping wine.

Even tho she knew better, Homegirl said, Give me a glass of wine.

That's when things went a little blurry.

Homegirl remembers Richboy opening a jug of cheap wine after Roomy's wine was gone and she and Richboy drinking it and getting Roomy to drink it, too, even tho she's a wine snob, supposedly. She remembers Roomy saying, I'm going to bed. She remembers hanging out with Richboy on his balcony. She remembers looking down and thinking about jumping or not jumping, but not thinking about either option very deeply and not caring either way. She remembers Richboy leading her into his bedroom or maybe she led him in. She remembers making out with Richboy and then she has no panties on and only her merry widow.

She remembers Richboy stopping and saying, The media has conditioned me.

She remembers stopping and almost sitting up and saying, The media has conditioned you what?

She remembers him saying something about how she's too big for him. Too fleshy or something. She vaguely remembers hitting him and he has his hands all over her curvy thighs and they are scuffling but in a kind of not good way.

It could go bad.

It could go good.

Then he's kissing her and saying something about joking or at least that's what she thinks he said for her to let him tie her up after that.

She's tied up and she lets him do whatever to her.

She's tied up and he finally puts his big cock in her and they fuck and she comes and she thinks something about him and how she wants to protect him from him and how she wants to protect him and how can she protect him and how can she protect him when she's got these rope restraints and how can she protect him.

He brings out a nurturing aspect in her that makes her want to punch him in the face.

She should have punched him in the face because that was the good part, the telling her she's fat and the tying up.

After that it goes bad.

After that, he asks her, at one point, Are you a bitch like all the other little bitches?

That's one of the few things she can remember. That and some woman, maybe Roomy, shoving something, some kind of plant – weed?, parsley? rosemary? thyme? – up her snatch.

Like she was Thanksgiving turkey.

Then she remembers weird dreams and/or weird chanting and shadows dancing and genuflecting and she's tied up again and was she ever untied and she tried to give Richboy head and that's when he said the bitch thing or maybe she tried to give him head later cos he was fisting Roomy and she was jealous but if she was tied up how could she even reach.

She remembers missing Punkboy. She remembers wanting him to protect her, somehow. She remembers wishing she'd told him and not Richboy; she remembers wanting him to be a daddy. And she remembers waking up in the morning and she was sick and bruised but free and Richboy and Roomy were nowhere and she knew they were gone; & she knew she was hurt and she knew she was hurting and bleeding and she knew the fetus, his fetus, their fetus, the one she'd told him about earlier this week, the one she was gonna stop drinking for, that fetus was gone.

SEVENTEEN

Who am I and how do I know all this shit? How do I know what Homegirl remembers and what she don't? How do I know what Richboy and Roomy really did, how they drugged and ritualized and aborted and fucked as she bled?

How Roomy was never really a roommate?

How the plants she stuffed up Homegirl's snatch was really a bundle of parsley?

How they hurt Homegirl and planned beforehand on hurting her?

I AM META!!!

META META META META! MEET ME! META! MEET>MEAT I AM! META!

Who is Meta's meta?

I AM!

I'm in control of all this shit.

I AM META! I AM. META. MEAT. META!

Meet me.

& I tried to meet Homegirl the other night, a couple of nights before the bad shit went down, before the shit I didn't know was gonna go down went down. I mean, I tried to make myself known to her; I mean, I tried to make her know me as a person the way I know her. I want to be in her life for reals.

We were at the dive bar and it was Punkboy's night cos Homegirl's smart enough to never let the two cross paths. Richboy's tried to get her to go with him to the dive bar but she's always been able to distract him. She's got perfect breasts, she does, even if a certain someone says she's too curvy for him. That may have something to do with it.

And, like I said, Punkboy wasn't there and Homegirl was there alone waiting for him, even one of her trusty disposable girlfriends couldn't be wrangled up this night cos it was a Wednesday. Homegirl was drinking Beam and Cokes and getting wasted cos the bartender was her favetender and he poured her drinks whiskey with a coke-splashy; even tho he was a bigger casualty than Homegirl's roommate even he still remembered the way her cunt tasted.

I've always wanted to know for reals how good it was and as the hour got later, I got closer and closer to her sitting alone at the bar. I moved seat after seat to be nearer to her. I quit drinking my beers so I could have my wits about me.

There is nothing so romantic and wrong and sexy as a hot woman sitting alone at a bar.

There is nothing so romantic and wrong as someone like me desperate in love.

I finally was sitting next to her and she seemed drunk so I offered her a cigarette cos I knows her and I know she only smokes when she's drunk.

Thanks, she said. And she took that cigarette between her lips and would it be a huge cliché to say I thought about her taking something else between her lips?

Yes, yes it would.

I always takes it too far when I likes someone.

I am needier and yearninger for love than Homegirl sometimes and I can appreesh her yearning, and I can hate it, too.

Need a light, I said, cos I'm sauve like that.

She acquiesced and bent towards me and I got to look down her shirt at her black bra and her nipples poking through the lace of the cups and I didn't want that brief flicker to ever end.

Yeah, I'm a sucker.

Thanks, she said. Then she sat there and smoked and pretended to write in her moleskine.

I could tell she was only pretending to write cos her pen was not moving horizontally. Plus her moleskine was close enough for me to read and she wasn't writing anything except, What to do?, which she wrote about four times all in small letters.

I knew it had nothing to do with Punkboy and everything to do with Richboy. She'd told the Richboy and not the Punkboy and I don't know why and she don't know why. Maybe she wanted the Richboy to be the father. Maybe she thought the Punkboy was shooting blanks cos of all the gangas he smoked.

I let her finish her smoke and then an old Prince song came on and the other bartender, Georgieboy was falsettoing with the music and I said to Homegirl, My name's Meta.

I put my hand out for her to shake so she couldn't ignore me.

She shook my hand and said, Hi.

She didn't give me her name and I refused to take it as a sign. I have always been full of hope disproportionate.

Need another smoke?, I said.

Sure, she said.

I need your name, first, I said.

Homegirl, she said.

And your digits, I said.

Got a piece of paper?

No, I said. I didn't want to seem overeager. I did have papers on me.

She flagged Favetender down and got him to get her a scrap of paper and a pen even. She wrote in big cursive letters, Homegirl, and then her number, 606-0842.

Maybe I was too full of hope or beer to realize as she slipped me that scrap of paper. I gave her a smoke and lit it and then Punkboy magically appeared and ordered beers for both of them and there was a chair vacant for him of course on her other side and they drank a couple of beers and as they were heading out loudly and stumbly I called the number she'd given me and it was an old eighties song about waiting for you I remembered just then and I got some sex line and I swear I could then hear Homegirl sucking tongue with Punkboy just outside the door and so I left the bar and there they were in the bus shelter, right outside the bar. They hadn't even made it back to Punkboy's house and they were making out and Punkboy's hands were proprietarily all over Homegirl's tits and Homegirl's hands were all feminine rubbing his hair up and down and back and forth and she was kinda squirming and I watched for a coupla minutes and got really pissed and went home and masturbated angrily for like fifty minutes and didn't come, probably cos of the beers.

Meta tried to pick up this Homegirl chick at a bar but b*tch gave him the wrong number or else she was too drunk and couldn't remember her own cell number, which is a very good possibility.

Meta, like everyone else, easily gets bored with their own FB updates.

Meta is one of those FBers who comment on their own FB status updates. Not because Meta has no friends but because that's how Meta roll. Meta also doesn't find talking about Meta in the third person the least bit awkward.

Homegirl oh my god, my head.

Homegirl wants to know if you know any publishers or agents or even interns or an intern's intern or the people responsible for *Twilight*'s popularity. Or Goth minions looking for a mistress/author.

Homegirl is going to get a tatt that says "deirfiúr" and will tell anyone who asks it means "deflowered."

Meta likes **If you think writing about writing is so 1990, I will cut you, If you think meta-fiction's seen its day, I will kill your dog and also make every day of your life just slightly less pleasant by one unnoticeable increment til you gets to the point where your less pleasant day is your standard for pleasant,** and **I bet this pickle can get more fans than yo mama.**

Homegirl likes, **Omg, leave me alone, my head** and **Go get mama a highball and quit your crying cos Santa ain't real**.

EIGHTEEN

These are the things Homegirl doesn't remember; these are the things she saw as she lay tied up on that bed, not for a night, like she thought, but for almost 72 hours. She doesn't remember these hours; she doesn't remember being bruised and bleeding and crying and pleading.

Homegirl was alone in the darkness and that's all she felt.

The darkness pressed in on her and she wanted to fight it; she wanted to, but her legs and arms were tied to the huge wooden simulacrum of acorns that made up the bed posts. She would've punched the darkness, she would've clawed, kicked, scratched, slapped that darkness if she'd been free. If she could ever've been free.

The only thing she could do was spit at it, and she was so thirsty.

She'd had nothing to drink but alcohol and some drug concoction in her wine she'd thought was just wine.

She was alone in the darkness and she saw herself at eight with her buck teeth and those skinny little braids. She was followed through the darkness by a Quentinkid; he kicked her in the crotch and then pushed her down and gave her a facewash of darkness.

It was cold and dark and she tried not to cry, but she cried and the darkness melted a little, but then froze back up on her cold buck-toothed skinny face.

She was alone in the darkness with a guy that looked like a

muscley Clark Kent. A guy she'd been trying to repress. A guy that she let push his dick up her ass who said he'd stop if it was too much but wouldn't stop after she said, No more. It'd felt like he was breaking something inside her.

She tried to throw that feeling back at the darkness but the darkness ate it up, smiled, belched, and then got darker for good measure.

She was alone with a man who looked like her father and they were throwing bowling balls at the darkness, but the darkness ate the balls and the darkness sent back bowling pins and then the man said something about how her fifteen year old breasts were real nice nice little titties.

She was alone in the darkness but then there was Labretboy and they were bowling and Labretboy was getting strikes and the scoreboard was going crazy every time. & every time the pins would fly off into the darkness, and Homegirl felt like crying she loved Labretboy's moves so much.

& the darkness was just a little bit less dark.

& Homegirl stopped pleading and only whimpered for a moment.

But then Homegirl was alone on the smoke-stank carpeted steps going down to Labretboy's basement bowling hangout/bar and it was because she and Labretboy always always fought when they weren't fucking and she tried to console herself that she was a weeble and weebles wobbled but they never fell down.

The darkness didn't care if she was standing or wobbling; the darkness didn't care and the darkness got darker. The darkness sucked up Labretboy and his pins, too, just to show her what's what.

She was alone with her fantasies about Richboy and these fantasies she'd tried so hard to repress, these fantasies she'd never expressed. How she wanted to marry him and when he'd come home from wherever he was, which wouldn't be work cos that just wasn't like him, she'd be wearing nothing but a seethrough something and she'd have a highball ready and she'd suck him off the minute he got in and if he didn't like it he might spank her and if he really didn't like it he might give her to the pizza boy and if he didn't like her he might cat o'nine tails her and if he really really didn't like it he wouldn't fuck her.

The withholding was always the worst.

She was alone with Peanutbuttersandwiches. Not the actual sandwich, but an artist she'd dated who'd make out with her and then have to leave because 1) he was allergic to something and/or 2) he had to eat a peanut butter sandwich. When he broke up with her, he'd said as her screen door slammed shut, I'll always love you.

She was alone in the darkness and that screen door kept slamming slamming slamming on her.

She was alone in the darkness but then she was outside a bar and she was with this other artist guy and she was drunk and there was a cute punky drunk standing by them and she invited the artist guy and the punky guy back to her house and she made them listen to her read her own poetry and it was a battle of the dicks and the nice artsy guy tried to wait it out but the punky guy had more stamina that way and then she was alone with the pierced tongued tattooed punky guy who was also an artist and who had a girlfriend and who couldn't get it up but went down on her with his pierced tongue and ruined for her all other oral sex ever and told her she tasted good and then a week later called her up for a threeway and then she never heard from him again until he turned into her favorite bartender/withholder.

She was alone in the darkness and her uterus was that screen door.

She was alone in the darkness and then there was the ex-Marine and she was buying cigarettes from him again at the Shell station and he was young and she was younger and foolish and he looked at her and she looked at him and for a moment there was a little bit of real real light.

Then she was alone in the darkness and the screen door was rasping against her other insides.

She was alone but then she wasn't. She was in the workshop again, on the first day and there was Richboy and he was so tall and so handsome with blue eyes and wavy brown hair, so handsome that she can only remember these vague details because if she remembers him in detail the screen door will cut into her heart.

The screen door will become her heart.

The screen door becomes her heart cos she can't forget him.

She's alone in the darkness and the june beetles are hurtling themselves at her screen, at the little bit of light she and the ex-Marine made.

She's alone and then there's the ex-Marine again and a pinball machine and she's pretending like she cares about pinball, but all she really cares about are how the lights go crazywild when he gets one in the hole.

She wants to be his pinball again; she wants to be his hole.

She's alone in the darkness of the tikki bar and then there's the ex-Marine and she's breaking up with him cos he, too, gots a girlfriend; she's got him by the leather lapels and it's so beautiful and so melodramatic that if she could freeze her life at this instant she just wouldn't go forward ever.

& that's when the lights really go out.

NINETEEN

These are more of those things I know that Homegirl doesn't.

Like I said, Roomy was never Richboy's roommate; they did meet on Craig's List, tho. He went looking for a bad witch. Roomy was a bad witch.

Richboy wanted to cover all his bases.

Roomy wasn't always bad.

Richboy wasn't always bad.

There are many reasons for both of their behaviors, and then again there are no reasons. Life's like that & most humans are pretty fucking fucked up.

Roomy grew up in a strict Baptist family, a dirt poor cliché.

Richboy grew up in a fractured, distant family, a rich as fuck cliché.

The two did fuck as Homegirl lay there bleeding. It was part of the ritual; plus, Roomy thought Richboy was hot and wanted more than anything to fuck him and as she fucked him she fantasized about fucking him in front of her Bible-beating mother.

Literally. Her mother beat her with the Bible.

She thought about filming it all, but even bad witches have sense enough not to incriminate themselves.

Richboy did film it all cos he just doesn't give a fuck. His rents will get him out of any trouble he gets himself into. His rents gave up on discipline and love years ago and now just

throw money at him whenever he needs them.
    Until he goes too far.
    He doesn't know yet what too far is.
    Shadow will show him.

TWENTY

Homegirl woke up and she was alone. She could tell she was alone cos she couldn't hear any live-living noises. Her arms were at her sides, but she couldn't really move them; all she could do was try to flop them. They felt like weird squiddy things; they barely felt attached to her. Her legs were folded up in the fetus position and she couldn't move them at all. All she could do was rock them a little, but even that slight movement made her say, fuck, fuck, fuck, fuck. Her guts hurt.

Her guts hurt a fuck of a lot.

She knew this was more than a hangover.

She wanted to touch her legs and make sure they were still working, try to unbend them or something, she wanted to touch her guts and make sure they were still in her, she wanted to touch her crotch cos she was laying in something wet and cold and she'd never pissed herself once, even those two times she got Toulouse-Lautrec shitfaced.

Homegirl liked to be in control even when she was out of control. She would hold onto that feeling of control even to the last possible minute of her black-out, of her sleep, of her orgasm. Anything.

Homegirl was getting freaked out cos she was feeling out of control and not just cos of the drink. She knew there was more to it than that and all she wanted to do was touch her limbs each to each and touch her abdomen and touch her cunt and touch her womb.

Her womb.

That's when she remembered what she woke up trying to forget.

She started to cry. Her crying shook her body and made her insides hurt more, which made her cry more. She couldn't stop. She was crying hard and sounds were coming out of her she didn't know she could make; sounds were coming out of her she hadn't even guessed existed somewhere within her. Sounds were coming out. Sounds were coming out and she couldn't stop them. Primal fucking sounds. Sounds that, had she been thinking logically or not been in so much pain, would have made her think about Cro-Magnons or Neanderthals and trying to keep a fire going and not knowing how to start a fire and it's raining and the baby at her dug's dying from cold, or being a bonobo and having her lover snatched and brained by rival aggro-chimps. Beasty, earthy, eerie, ancient fucked up sounds of pain and lost.

Homegirl was keening almost and didn't hear whoever it was come in.

Homegirl was crying and it hurt to cry, like I said, and there were tears all over and mucous and spit, and her face was all red and contorted and grimacy and lined, but like we're gonna look down on her for not looking beautiful as she cries.

It's like looking hot when you come. No one does it but porn stars; no one cries pretty pretty except Hollywood starlets.

Someone was approaching the bed; even over her sobs, she

could hear him or her creak the wood floor. She got as ready as she could; she tried to make a fist. She almost made a fist.

Homegirl flopped her arm out and smacked whoever it was with a floppy tentacley arm thingy.

Ouch, the person said.

Homegirl wanted to roll over, but couldn't. She knew that voice and knew it wasn't Richboy, like she'd been afraid it'd be, or Roomy, who she'd like to have a go at when her limbs weren't acting like weird B movie sci-fi extras or beached whales or something but I'm having trouble getting across the simile cos the closest I've ever come to floppy arms like Homegirl's is when I've slept on my arms for like nine hours at the most, not 72.

I could make a joke about the masturbatory potential of Homegirl's hands here, but that would just be wrong, given the circumstances and all, and you'd probably start to hate me, if you haven't already.

Goddamn, the voice said.

Then the voice said, Homegirl? & the voice now sounded urgent.

Homegirl said, Punkboy.

TWENTY-ONE

Now you're probably all like, what the fuck is this? I didn't sign up for no Gothic romance bullshit: Homegirl – the damsel in distress, and Punkboy – the Byronic hero. Fuck you, Meta, fuck you, is what you're saying.

I can hear you, bitches.

I lied, tho. I don't control it all. I couldn't stop Punkboy from realizing Homegirl'd never not shown up for work without finding someone to sub for her and that Homegirl'd never dropped off the radar so entirely or from somehow knowing his roommate *was* a creeper who creeped around in a creepy way creeping after Homegirl all through Riverwest and all through the East side, creeping creeping in his 1974 pea-green Impala or from asking creepy creeper where he'd last seen her. & I didn't really want to stop Punkboy from that realization. In fact, I might have goaded him into it…

Would I be making it better if I told you Punkboy was a serial killer in the making and that as a child he'd practiced on rodents then turtles then birds then dogs but not cats cos he will always and forever love cats and then badgers cos they're the meanest little fuckers and that when he sees Homegirl all beat and bloody his serial killerness comes out and he picks her up and carries her out of the bedroom all the way to his house over five blocks in the dead of night just to tie her up and slowly cut her up?

If it does then you're a sick bloody fuck and if it turns you

91

on you should go see someone about that, most definitely.

And it ain't going down like that.

Punkboy accidentally shot a squirrel with a bb gun when he was a kid and it died and he cried and his older behemoth half-brother smacked him upside the head and told him not to be such a pussy.

This didn't lead to any serial killerness in Punkboy, tho. His brother'd be more likely; his brother sociopathes often.

Plus, Punkboy didn't carry her all the way to his house; he carried her to her car and put her gently in it and then he got in and he motherfucking drove for like the third time in his motherfucking life. For reals.

& I probably shoulda tipped Punkboy off earlier but I was pissed about those fake digits Homegirl gave me and I didn't know what was going down with Richboy and Roomy, either. I did ask about Homegirl at the café. I did. I ain't lying.

You've got no choice but to believe me.

It went down like this:

Punkboy was pissed cos he got caught at the counter by me when he went up to put some Black Flag cos it was punk rock but it was still okayed by the Man, the once punk rock owner of the café who'd been gentrified, on the stereo and I knew he was pissed and I'd waited until he'd gone up there and then while he was bending over to put the CD in I hurried to the counter with my pint glass and my fitty cents for a refill.

Punkboy stood up and saw me and didn't even try to smile. He just took the pint with his tattoed hand and began to fill it up.

Where's that tall bangy girl who cooks sometimes?, I said.

Punkboy pretended not to hear me.

I haven't seen that tall girl in a while, I said.

Punkboy pushed the pint glass at me and hit buttons on the register.

Is she on vacation?, I asked.

He took my money and said, Why? What's it to you?

I looked at him as I picked up my pint; I didn't say anything. I could see things forming in his head. Things like did he have to kick my ass and was I a stalker and things like where was Homegirl and why hadn't she sexted him lately or met up with him at the bar and they hadn't fucked in three days and had she found someone else but she'd still come to work, wouldn't she?

She had that goddamned Midwestern work ethic and Punkboy knew she'd goddamned come to work or find someone to cover before letting anyone at the café down.

Punkboy grabbed some of Casualty's emergency dank dank buds from the spice jar in the kitchen and went out back to the alley for a spliff and a think. Sandwiches and salads and hungry yuppie punk-wannabes could wait; this shit was important.

TWENTY-TWO

Punkboy didn't scoop Homegirl up in his arms and carry her home right away; Punkboy wanted to call an ambulance.

You've got blood. Dried blood all over your legs, he said.

There's blood on the sheets. Fuck, he said. And he was suddenly very angry and suddenly he got an image of his half-brother's head exploding from a shotgun blast and didn't know where the hell that'd come from.

He wanted to blow shit up right now. Lots of shit, buildings, cars, brothers, beds, railroad tracks, stoplights, arthouse theatres, whoever did this. He wanted to watch everything around him explode and he wanted to explode the rubble left after the explosions and explode the atoms of the rubble and the quarks of the atoms and the whatevers of the quarks until there was nothing left but a fine dust covering him and Homegirl and nothing else.

He was sitting next to Homegirl on the bed. He was holding her up; she was having trouble sitting up. She was also having trouble focusing, and talking felt weird.

I just want out, she said.

What?

I just want out of here, Homegirl said. Her throat was so dry. She could barely move her tongue; it felt like a wild animal trapped in her mouth, a wild animal that was laying low, waiting for the hunters that'd ensnared it so it could rip their motherfucking throats out. The laying low, the sinking down felt intentionally cruel yet careful.

You're hurt, Punkboy said.

Homegirl wanted to say, duh, but didn't have it in her. She had nothing in her; she felt like she'd float off and the only thing keeping her tethered was Punkboy's wiry arm around her shoulder. She felt like if she was taken to a hospital she would float off; float off into some stratosphere and burn up or fall to the earth with a thud. She felt like she couldn't face a night alone in a strange bed with rough hospital linen and gruff nurses and old people exhaling old people smells and old people lives, dying breaths and dead loves and whiny kids and crying spouses and all those peopley things she was forever running away from condensed into five plus floors, condensed to pure essence of human comi-tragedy or tragi-comedy or whatever the fuck it was. All those people just wanting to breathe and keep breathing and their progeny either wanting that or wanting them to die and there's no in between in a hospital and Homegirl just couldn't stand it. She was in between; she would always be in between.

No hospital, she said.

Punkboy looked at her and nodded. He would make sure she got to some kind of doctor tomorrow. Tonight he would clean her and feed her and hold her so she could sleep. He could tell she couldn't be alone.

For a punker he could be kind of sensitive, even tho his half-brother'd tried all his childhood to pound that out of him; that sensitivity was another one of his dirty little secrets, but he didn't worry too much about it, he hid it well behind tattoos and alcohol and skateboards and grindcore.

I'll take you home, he said.

TWENTY-THREE

Cos he never wore pajamas, cos he was pretty much anti-pajamas, Punkboy crawled nakedly and quietly out of bed, careful not to wake Homegirl up. She hadn't fallen asleep until the birds'd started chirping and he'd stayed awake with her, even tho it'd been hard. He'd held her and waited and waited until he finally felt her relax a little, until her muscles unclenched and he could hear her breathing. She sometimes snored and sometimes he cared but now he wanted to hear her snoring. He knew, tho, it would take a long time until she relaxed like that again, and then he fell asleep, too.

He waked and baked and then called in to work; he also tried calling the café owners to get Homegirl her job back. He left a message; he knew they never answered the office phone. They were always out drinking or doing something fabulous with their days. Speeding on Ducatis down Miltown streets no one else knew existed or picking up supermodels from the airport on said Ducatis or whatever, things Punkboy couldn't imagine.

Richboy could, of course. He moved in those same kind of circles when he wasn't full of complete and utter self-loathing and slumming it with girls like Homegirl. Richboy had serious rich white privileged boy tortured soul issues and didn't expect anyone else in the world to understand him. He was misunderstood and that's why he did what he did.

Whatever. Even I think he's a prick and not just cos of

the way I feel about Homegirl. But you probably think I'm a prick so my opinion don't count.

That's how it works, eh?

Punkboy got off the phone and thought very briefly how he hadn't seen his roommate since he'd interrogated him about his creepy-creeping ways. But this thought went away as he looked around trying to remember what it was he'd been looking for in his living room, what he needed to bring back to his bedroom, besides the phone and besides another spliff. He sat down on the couch to think.

It took a while.

He thought about explosions again for a while.

He thought about his half-brother and how he'd always looked up to him when he was a pre-teen and would tag along to lameass things like Judas Priest concerts and get wasted in the parking lot with Bigbrother before the show and he'd try to be a man and hold his liquor so Bigbrother would notice how much he respected him and wanted to be like him but he always woke up, alone, passed out on cold black asphalt still in the goddamned parking lot and the concert'd be over and his half-brother'd be halfway across town at some chick's house fucking the Judas out of her.

He grabbed the yellow pages and went back to his bedroom; he was gonna find Homegirl a doctor. He was gonna assess the damage done. He got into bed and snuggled up against her under the covers.

Yes, even punkboys snuggle.

He felt her soft skin against him and of course, he got a boner and he wanted to do deep dicking things with her; he wanted to do ass and clit licking things to her, so he thought about explosions and Bigbrother and the way the parking lot girls at the Judas Priest concerts would kinda mock him and kinda be nice to him as they passed him the Goldshlager bottle and commanded him to chug.

They were always feeling sorry for him and never wanting to fuck him.

Of course, he'd been only twelve. But he could still appreciate, he had appreciated their big buoyed by bras breasts or their perky free ones and the pretty young faces underneath the tramp make-up and big hair.

Memories of their pity always deboned him. He opened the Yellow Pages and looked up clinics. He decided on Planned Parenthood cos he knew they were respectable and he got out from under the covers and called Planned Parenthood and didn't know what to say but knew to talk in a soft voice so as not to wake Homegirl when the woman's voice answered so he asked her their hours and she said they had many men's sexual health services and would he like to know about them and he said, no, thanks, just the hours and she gave him the hours and then said they had free condoms and he thanked her and tried not to think about what'd he need condoms for with Homegirl but he did start to think about those things and he could feel his cock swelling so before the woman's voice could hang up he asked her to tell him about the men's sexual health services so he could get his dick under control a second time quick and she read from a list that included std screenings (limper), infertility screenings (harder), erectile dysfunction services (and he felt himself going limper), prostate cancer screenings (he got harder), jock itch exams (softer), and vasectomies (harder), and overall that didn't help, so he thanked her and hung up.

Then he went to the bathroom and beat off. He imagined Homegirl as the GP and she was giving him a prostate exam and then she pretended to look at the chart and then she said, I'm a naughty GP cos he'd had one two months ago and didn't need one and then he had to spank her and then they were fucking on the floor of the exam room cos they couldn't even make it onto the examining table.

He came quick and hard.

He rested a moment & then flushed. Bon voyagey, he said to his little boys.

They didn't say anything back cos they're sperm and only have one goal – to penetrate that egg. That is all.

Punkboy's goal was to get Homegirl to the doctor today and also try to talk her into talking to the po, even tho like all punkboys the world over he hated the po.

It was that or go all vigilante on the fucker, whoever the fuck he was.

TWENTY-FOUR

It was day and Homegirl'd finally woken up and Punkboy got her dressed and dressed himself and then asked her if she wanted anything to eat or drink.

Homegirl said, Water.

So Punkboy brought her water and she drank it fast and deep, so fast and deep that all of a sudden she was coughing and all of a sudden it was coming up out her nose. Punkboy grabbed the glass from her and put it on the nightstand – yes, even punkboys have nightstands – and then Homegirl was crying and shaking and Punkboy was holding her and trying to comfort her.

Punkboy said, after she'd stopped shaking so much, We need to get you to a doctor.

Homegirl just nodded.

Punkboy said, Ready?

Homegirl leaned against him and then pulled away. Yes, she said.

Punkboy helped Homegirl up and then he supported her down the hallway and down the stairs and out the door of his house and he was so goddamned glad he didn't run into the creepy creeper of his roommate cos he was afraid he would try to take out his anger on that big motherfucker and that motherfucker was big and mean.

He was also afraid if he ran into his roommate he would get pissed that that dumb creepy creeper motherfucker hadn't

101

done anything to stop this.

If Punkboy even knew about me, I'd be toast.

Motherfucking toast. Yeah. That's what I'd be. Melba toast teethed to nothing by a vacant infant. Or toast that'd been margarined and then food-processered liquified toast and then that liquid toast'd be poured down the gullet of a hog and then that hog'd be split in half and I'd somehow be lodged somewhere that'd be split in half til I was fed to something else then split in half then fed then split ad infinitum.

He put Homegirl into the passenger side of her car. He was gonna drive again and he wasn't gonna care this time cos he was just stoned enough and it was daylight and he had to get Homegirl to a doctor and make sure she was gonna be okay.

He wanted her to be okay.

The Planned Parenthood he took her to was only about five blocks away; the same distance he'd had to drive last night, but in the other direction. Planned Parenthood was in what looked like the beginning of a strip mall – there were three stores: a sub shop, a closed-up shop with boards and everything, and Planned Parenthood. There was a check into cash kiddy corner to this little strip, and a rundown apartment complex next to that.

He parked and then helped Homegirl out of the car. They walked up the stairs, Punkboy's arm around her waist. He opened the outside door for her and then tried the inside glass door; it was locked.

There was a telephone with a notice saying something about everyone's protection and how to get in you had to call the front desk at all times.

This pissed Punkboy off. Seriously. What kind of fucking country did they live in that people who needed help, especially the poor, the downtrodden, the fucked up and abused people, had to go through this kind of shit to get it? It was another reason to add to his list of why he would always and forever be punk rock and why he might one day join the black balaclavaed anarchists smashing the corporate windows of the world. & he knew this was nothing, really, this having to call to get access to help through these glass doors was nothing compared to other people's things. It was just symbolic and it started a whole bunch of rage and exploding things and deep thinking things and he was imagining the lead singer of Judas Priest sticking dynamite up his half-brother's ass and calling it a hummer, he was imagining doing worse things to whoever did this shit to Homegirl and Homegirl musta sensed this cos she grabbed his free hand with her hand and squeezed and said, Please.

He picked up the phone. It rang. He could see the woman at the desk and she was not answering and he was trying not to get pissed at her now. It rang more.

It rang more.

Finally, the woman, without looking at the door, picked up and said, Yes?

Punkboy took a breath and said, Hello?

Deskwoman said, Do you have an appointment?

Punkboy said, No, I called earlier. They said I didn't need one.

Deskwoman said, Are you here for men's health?

Punkboy said, No. I think my girlfriend was assaulted.

There was a buzzing sound and the door opened immediately. Punkboy hung up the phone and walked Homegirl up to the desk.

Deskwoman said, Do you want me to call the police?

Homegirl said, I wasn't assaulted.

Deskwoman clicked her tongue.

Deskwoman said, Do you want a rape kit?

Homegirl said, I wasn't assaulted. I do want to see a doctor, tho.

Deskwoman said, Why?

Punkboy did not like Deskwoman's bedside manner or whatever you'd call it. Bitch was curt.

Homegirl said, I think I've miscarried. I think I've lost my baby…

Homegirl pulled away from Punkboy and started crying silently.

Punkboy felt like someone'd punched him in the gut. He knew that was a cliché but that's what it motherfucking felt like, a-ight?

Deskwoman said, I need you to fill these out, and thrust a clipboard with papers at Homegirl.

Homegirl took the clipboard and started walking over to a chair in the lobby without Punkboy; Punkboy was still kinda sagging against the wall by the window like he was the one who'd been assaulted, like he was the one whose body'd been messed with. Deskwoman gave him a look; he didn't move.

Deskwoman said, Can I help you?

And Punkboy thought, Yes, I'm gonna take out all my anger and hatred on your fugly bureaucratic face. I am gonna pound your face through that plate glass protective door until everyone who needs help can get in without your judgy face looking at them.

But Punkboy knew better than to say this cos he wanted someone to help Homegirl and he wanted to be there when someone helped her and made sure she was all right.

But... a baby!

He'd never wanted kids, but a baby...

Punkboy said, No. He went and sat down next to Homegirl in the small empty lobby. Some movie was playing on the VCR/TV combo attached to the wall but there was no sound and all Punkboy could think was, Babybabyexplosionsmotherfuckerbabybabymotherfucker iwillfuckyouupkillingababyidontwantbabiesthoughtabouta vasectomybutstillmotherfucker was that my motherfucking baby?

Homegirl kept writing things on the clipboard as Punkboy thought these things and the soundless movie – it might have been *Caddyshack* or it might have been the tot inappropriate *For Keeps* or it might have been Goddard's *Breathless* or it might have been Sartre or Yahweh or some deity revealing the reason for existence, who knows cos no one was watching that shit – played on the TV attached to the wall.

Homegirl got up and returned the clipboard to Deskwoman.

Punkboy tried not to think about what she'd been through and what she'd lost.

They waited and did not talk. They waited in hard plastic chairs next to each other. They waited and did not touch. They waited and neither of them found anything to focus on.

Not even the movie.

Which turned out to be the 1990 *Teenage Mutant Ninja Turtles*. Maybe it was supposed to be calming.

Nursepractitioner came out and called, Homegirl and Homegirl got up and Punkboy got up.

& Homegirl said, You wait here.

& Punkboy said, But…

& Homegirl said, Please wait here for me.

& Punkboy didn't say anything but he knew this was a mistake on Homegirl's part and he knew she would need him and she would need him even after this and he didn't know if he was up for that and part of him wanted to say, hell no, I'm coming with you, and part of him wanted to say, Okay, and wait for her to get in the examining room and then somehow get through the next locked door and then knock on her examining room door like the doctor and then she'd have to let him in, and a big part of him wanted to say, Okay, and then wait for her to go down that locked corridor, wait for her to be out of sight and to get the fuck out of that place as fastfuck as he could and to just keep going. Walk as far and as fast as he could from that place. Walk to the nearest dive bar and commence drinking and to drink as fast and far as he could.

He'd walk cos he wasn't a complete dick and he couldn't strand Homegirl here, not after what'd happened to her.

He'd leave the keys with the judgy bitch there.

Of course he stayed and of course he waited and Homegirl came out and he could tell she'd been crying again and when she saw him she kinda fell into him and she started bawling and she said, I'm most likely infertile now.

Okay, she wasn't that eloquent cos she was bawling and shit.

She said, I prob...

She said, I can't...

She said, They think...

& they were still in that teenage mutant yellowplastic chaired lobby and judgy Deskwoman was there at the desk watching and not even pretending not to watch and Punkboy wanted to go up to that glass partition and bump against it with his body and be all like, What? What, bitch, what? What, bitch. I will FUCK YOU UP. I will FUCK YOU UP if you don't stop staring with your little beady judgy eyes. I will sodomize you with a mangosteen dick and grapefruit balls. I will earfuck you with a steamroller and I will eyefuck you with a steamshovel. I will not touch your moldy vag, judgy bitch.

He didn't, tho, cos he couldn't let go of Homegirl cos she woulda fallen to the floor.

Homegirl said, No babies.

Homegirl said, I can't.

Punkboy held her and stared at Deskwoman who was still staring at them. She was probably thinking judgy thoughts about pierced tatted people who don't love god and who don't have jobs and who are a drain on the system and how she only had a couple more weeks left in this den of sin before she went to work for the pharmacy where she'd never have to prescribe ru-486 cos it was against her new principles.

Bitch kept staring back; Homegirl was crying crying and

Punkboy, well, Punkboy kept his cool better than I'd expected.

Punkboy said, What the fuck are you looking at?

Then Punkboy said, What. The. Fuck. Are you. Looking. At.

Deskwoman didn't say anything; she pretended she had to answer the phone.

TWENTY-FIVE

Homegirl was kneeling on her bed in that goddamned merry widow with the blood stains still; she'd been wearing the thing every day since Punkboy'd driven her home the day after Planned Parenthood and he was kinda getting the hang of this driving thing; it'd been so much better than the other night when he'd driven bloodied, beat up Homegirl to his house and worried the whole time he was gonna get pulled over cos he didn't have a license and didn't really know how to drive, he knew the brake and the accelerator, but he didn't know the nuances, and then the po would think he'd done *that* to Homegirl and take him in and never let him out. That was one of his biggest fears, prison, captivity, not being allowed to get up and go whenever and wherever he wanted to.

Since then, Punkboy'd stayed over every night for the past two weeks at Homegirl's, except last night. He'd gotten the café manager to give him a whole bunch of day shifts so he could get to Homegirl's house by seven at night and cook her dinner. He didn't think she ate when he wasn't around. He'd had to work a night shift last night and so hadn't stayed the night, but got his tired ass up at eight in the morning to walk over and see her and cook her breakfast if she was in the mood. He sat next to her on her bed and wondered if he should suggest breakfast, then wondered what she did all day when he wasn't there and then he thought, this, this is what she does, this is what she does all day when I'm not here, what's she doing now, this picking through her split ends thing, this minute examination of small clumps of hair, this pulling of the ends apart, this.

And there's something so incongruous and wrong about a hot young woman whose perky tits are almost popping out of her lingerie with her head bent, cross-eyed, fingers obsessing the ends of her hair. Add to that the blood stains on the bottom of her jaunty little skirt and Punkboy felt sick to his stomach like he used to when he went through that really bad ulcer spell and tried to solve the pain by drinkingdrinking and drinking so much he started puking up coffeegrounds blood; he didn't know how much more of this he could take.

He wanted to be there for her, but he was also now wanting to get the hell away from her. He didn't understand why she was doing what she was doing, why she was doing nothing, and why especially, even with his hatred for the Man, she never called the cops and got that fucker arrested. He couldn't take what he was reading as passivity, it didn't seem like the Homegirl he knew and loved to fuck so well. Yeah, she liked to be submissive sometimes in bed, but sometimes, goddamn, she'd climb on top with her boots still on and get in charge. There was no get in charge vibe here; there was only hurt and wallowing and it sucked and it made him want to hurl pint glasses and beer bottles and whiskey bottles and plates and mirrors against her wall until she stopped pulling on her hair ends and looked at him and said, Stop. Or better yet, Yes.

Yes. Don't stop. And she would join in and they would hurl shit against her bedroom wall and they would be crazy and youngish again and when they ran out of shit to hurl they would run down the sidewalk with bats and smash things randomly like car windows and mailboxes and bus shelters and street signs and the goddamned pavement why not? and then duck into an alleyway for a quickie up against a two car garage door and he would lift her up and she would say, Yes, don't stop and then she would be saying those fuck things he loved to hear so much and then she would be moaning and wailing so loud and so long that the whole neighborhood would hear that shit in their sleep and wake up crying without knowing why but subconsciously knowing it was cos they were never gonna fuck like that for the rest of their lives and this was something, this was the fear the whole neighborhood tried to keep at bay by buying two cars and planting sunflowers and getting promotions and procreating more and more babies and going to Disneyworld and having over a hundred choices of jogging strollers to choose from.

He would never want any of that; this is what he wanted: the yes, don't stop against all the garage doors of the world.

What he didn't know and what Homegirl didn't even know was that she wanted something else entirely right now, that she was doing this to push him away. She didn't know this but she needed to be alone to regroup, to filter, to re-collect her inner things, to get those pieces of her that were stuck in the darkness back somehow. She needed Punkboy the most now and so she was pushing him away cos humans are perverse like that and that's how it is. When you really really need to rely on someone, when you know they get you and they'll be there for you, is when you push them away cos you don't want to show weakness or it seems too easy or it seems too easy so there must be some ulterior motive or you're just fucked up or cos someone did it to you once or whatever.

You know I'm not talking about you, anyway cos you don't do shit like that, especially if you've never been laid properly or had your heart flattened by a steam roller of a man or woman or had that fauxfriend give you drugs and perform black magic rites to induce a miscarriage or just had him or her tell you you were too damn fat to fuck.

Too fat too fat too fat to fuck...

Shit, I know this is grownup serious time now and you probably hate me now even more than you did before; I just couldn't resist the allusion, and if you don't get it, if you don't know *Too Drunk to Fuck* (I'll even give ya the Nouvelle Vague cover) then I motherfucking know you ain't never drunk wrestled and there ain't never gonna be the glimmer of that in your dullassgottagetuptomakethemoneyforthefamily thathatesmeandohmygodI'maclicheofaclicheI'mworsethan thatprincipalfromthe*BreakfastClub* eye.

Homegirl was going to figure out what to do about Richboy and what he'd done to her, to her body, and she was gonna do it alone.

Plus she felt so super guilty about not even telling Punkboy about the baby that she can't even deal with the fact that she didn't tell him. She may never tell him cos she doesn't know how to tell him now.

She may hate Punkboy foreverever for abandoning her, tho, even tho that's what she secretly subconsciously deepdown wants right now.

Cos that's how humans work, too.

I don't know why I even try sometimes.

Punkboy started a fight with Homegirl, of course.

What are you doing?, he said.

What? She still had a clump of hair pulled down in front of her eyes; she was still rooting through the ends for splits.

Punkboy grabbed both of her hands. This made her feel something for a sec and she did not like it. She looked at Punkboy for the first time since he'd gotten there. He was so close and she could smell that he'd taken a shower recently and she could hear him breathing, but she didn't want to suck his breath in. She didn't want to be reminded of breathing.

Let me go, Homegirl said.

Punkboy didn't. Let's call the cops; let's get the fucker. He was now caressing her hands, the soft insides of her wrists; there were no scars there and he wanted to keep it that way.

Homegirl didn't answer; she just shifted her body so she was no longer kneeling, but had her legs curled up underneath her.

Fuck. We need to call the po. C'mon, Punkboy said.

Why?, Homegirl said.

Cos, it'll make you feel better. He was still rubbing her wrists softly softly.

Homegirl pulled her hands away and then even moved away from Punkboy. How do you know what'll make me feel better?

Maybe she was the one looking for a fight.

Yeah, right, I already told you she was.

Punkboy said, I don't. I just…

What?

Want to help, he said.

Help? Help? Homegirl got off the bed, tossed her split ends out of her face. What makes you think I need help?

Punkboy wanted to hurl bombs at this point; wanted to hurl bombs at his half-brother and whoever did this and all the other fuckers in the world who got off on causing someone a huge motherfucking amount of pain, we're talking real sadists here, a little bit of pain, some gossip, a break-up, a broken heart, a job termination, a small humiliation, was nothing compared to this shit. His hurled bombs would be Molotov cocktails first then grenades then land mines then huge mortars and if that didn't wipe out those fuckers he would go steal a goddamned nuclear bomb from North Korea or some shit.

He wanted to see their faces melting melting; he wanted to record their melting faces and show them to Homegirl, replay the meltingfaces over in slo mo, play the meltingfaces backwards, montage the meltingfaces to D.R.I. or Napalm Death. But, he said nothing.

Help? Homegirl was almost screeching now. She had the roots of her hair in her hands now and looked like she was trying to pull it all off at the crown; she was all cliché Ophelia and Punkboy never wanted to be Hamlet.

Yes, Punkboys read, too.

Punkboy couldn't take seeing her like this; he got off that bed and left.

TWENTY-SIX

While Homegirl was splitting her ends, she was actually thinking deep thinking things. She was considering options and thinking and it looked like she wasn't thinking and it looked like she was vacant, pretty vacant, and if I were Postmodern I'd hyperlink right now to some fucking Sex Pistols just cos & also to see if you were surprised at all.

Cos if you were you're a baby and how did you get this far?

Homegirl's on that bed, still. She went back to her kneeling on the bed. She went back to kneeling in her bloody lingerie and it's so S&M that if I were a man I'd get a hard-on and if I were a woman I'd get some lady wood and if I were both I'd be ostracized by "normal" society.

Fuckers.

I will try to keep my commentary to a minimum.

Seriously.

Sorry. I have gotten bolder; I know.

It has something to do with being rejected and I don't really know what. There's prolly some mathematical equation for how putting one's self out there + rejection = more extroverted motherfuckers. Rejection + rejection + rejection = a nation of confessional poets blogging blogging blogging *listen to me. I've done much worse things than you could ever think up...*

Homegirl's been thinking, like I said.

Homegirl's been thinking about killing Richboy.

Homegirl's been thinking about killing Richboy but she

hasn't yet decided how she'll do it, she's thinking handgun, most likely, if she does. She can get one easily. It is America, after all.

She can buy one legally, but she thinks Punkboy's roommate has connections.

So she's got that figured out; she's worried about other things. They're not quite moral either.

She's pretty much beyond morals. She's just had her fetus and womb ripped out, without her permission.

Mostly she's been thinking about the ramifications. What comes after.

After she pulls the trigger (or however she tries to kill him) and there's a click and there's a meeting of the whatever with the whatever that propels the bullet down the grooved chamber, Homegirl doesn't know how guns work, she's only held a gun once very briefly in her life and not on purpose, and the bullet goes through Richboy's pretty forehead cos Homegirl's a lucky shot, Homegirl drops the gun or she conceals it in her boot or she takes it to the bar with her or she licks its hot smoking barrel and it burns her tongue to remind her. Never.

Never again.

And she thinks about getting a tattoo that says this somewhere on her body, but she doesn't have time cos she's just killed someone and she's gotta go on the run.

She knows this, even in her merrywidowing, splitending spaceout.

She'll go on the run and maybe she'll shave her head and it'll be like that 1985 movie about Billie Jean King, the tennis star, but she knows it wasn't about Billie Jean King, she's just having fun with herself cos it distracts her from the real questions of should I kill this worthless human who stole my baby and my reproductive abilities and if I do, how am I gonna get away with it.

He stole Homegirl's abilities to ever have babies and it's still sinking in.

She probably wouldn't have even kept his baby after the surprise, the mystery and novelty of being knocked up wore off. Like she was really gonna quit drinking.

She was young and she was food service. Nuff said.

But to have the choice taken from you was bullshit. More than bullshit. Fucked up shit.

And to have the choice of ever having anyone else's kids taken from you was more than fucked up. It was fucked up fucked-upness. It was quintessential fucked-upness. It was the Ozzie and Harriet of fucked-upness.

Tho Homegirl might not get that reference.

She wishes she were a cutter; she'd cut the date the baby died, and also when any chance she'd ever have to ever have a baby died into the soft folds of her labia and into her arm and into her stomach and her forehead. Everywhere. Bodily present. The body fucked with, the body fucked, the body hurt, the body remembered, the body vengeance.

She could kill him. She knows she could.

& if she did maybe she could become a legend, too. Not like the Garp legend where instead of their tongues now the women would cut out their uteruses to protest what happened to her uterus, but like Billie Jean. Where people shave their heads like her and/or know the po are chasing her across the nation and so they get her name tattooed somewhere conspicuous so she'll see it and they'll only hang at dive bars cos the cops don't hang there and she'll only hang at dive bars cos that's where she feels comfortable anyway and she'll see her name tattooed on an arm or a hand or a neck or an eyelid and she'll know she's found safe haven. Her army of yearners. She'll know they'll hide her and take care of her for as long as they can cos what Richboy did, taking away her choice of having their baby and then taking away her choice of having any babies, interfering with her body, trying to master her body cos her heart wasn't enough and killing the fetus wasn't enough, this ain't no "pro-life" shit, Homegirl's tattooed followers are mostly pro-choice and they're pissed cos she was given no choice, she was tied up and drugged and aborted and sterilized and it was a lot like rape and cos she's a woman you know her past history would come into play in court just like a rape victim and cos she's a barista-woman and Richboy's a richboy all Homegirl's food service punk rock and altrock and whatever-rock yearning army know he would win in court. Somehow.

Cos he's got the lawyers and he's got the law and he's got a dick and this is still a fucking patriarchal game no matter what.

Cos it's the game of Life and you win if you're a blue peg.

Cos if you're a pink peg you better get your ass married quick.

Cos Homegirl's a pink peg that likes the deepdicking and she's mostly not monogamous.

It's why Homegirl hasn't called the police.

It's why Homegirl fantasizes about shooting Richboy.

It's why Homegirl's fantasies don't include Punkboy; Punkboy may think Homegirl is oblivious sometimes but she knows him and she knows his fears. His fears are captivity; his fears are being out of control; his fears are not having a space to cook in and a space to clean or just even his own space.

It's why Homegirl's contemplating talking to the Shadow.

First, she's gonna pretend to get back to normal. She doesn't know if she'll ever feel normal again but she'll fake it til she makes it or some bullshit like that.

She calls the café office and gets the woman boss and she's happy she does cos the bitch is all business and she doesn't have to cry for her, she just tells her straight up that she was kidnapped and assaulted and she wants her job back.

& Businessbitch says, Yes. Okay.

& Businessbitch's thinking, We haven't replaced you yet and you pull in some customers with your long long legs, so yes, you can have your job back.

Homegirl gets off the phone feeling like she's got this pretending to be back to normal thing almost down.

She texts Punkboy, You home?

TWENTY-SEVEN

There could be a lot of reasons Punkboy didn't text her back: he wasn't home – he was at work or out skateboarding or something, he was pissed at her for reals, he was too stoned to figure out his cell again, or just cos. She was hoping it was the first and not the second. She waited a while to see if he'd text her back at all and then Homegirl got up, took a shower, put on lacy panties, a black tank, a cute little flippy skirt, and her knee-high ass-kicking boots, and went over to Punkboy's house.

She knocked on the door. There was no answer for a while; she was used to that.

Shadow opened the door and squinted out at her; he was only thirty something, but he looked fifty. Homegirl knew it was cos of the stuff he was rumored to have left behind when he moved here – mafia, drug cartel, snuff ring, dog fighting, child prostitution, no one really knew. He'd lived hard already and it'd left its mark.

Shadow had lived hard and dirty and he'd gotten out when he could. Not cos he found religion or love or morality or any of that Raskolnikov crap; he got out to save his skin. He had a slightly odd accent and told anyone who asked he was from Jersey, not that many did cos he gave off that don't ask me questions vibe that only idiots ignore. Jersey was probably why people thought mafia.

Russian mafia, maybe. Something Eastern European with

lots of fighting and killing.

He squinted at her some more and then said, Punkboy's not home.

Homegirl said, Oh.

Shadow made like he was gonna close the door. Homegirl said, Can I come in? Please?

Shadow felt that twinge he got in his neckroll when trouble was coming. He felt it and acknowledged it and then shook hands with it and lapped at it like a dog drinking water and then swooshed it around like a wine taster and thought, yes, that is the twinge, that is its balance and bouquet and tannin and finish, yes, aha, yes, and yet still opened the door.

Of course.

He held the door open for her and she came in. Homegirl's boots were noir seamed stockings to him. He wanted to give her a black hat with a veil and some Chanel red red lipstick and what the hell a 1930s Chanel black dress, too. Homegirl could feel his desire to give her things; Homegirl very much knew that feeling, she lived with that feeling always and this time she was gonna use someone else's need to give her things and this time she wasn't gonna feel guilty. She sat down on the black leather couch, which was Shadow's of course cos he's gots a thing for leather, without being asked, crossed her legs and stroked the leather of one boot from her ankle to her knee with one hand, then looked up at Shadow who was staring down at her. Shadow rubbed his neck and looked like he was having a quick, painful convo with himself.

Need a drink?, he said.

Whiskey, she said.

He rubbed his neck harder, then went to the hard alcohol stash he and Punkboy kept in a cabinet above the fridge. He came back with a bottle of Knob Creek and two glasses of ice and set them down on the coffee table.

You pour, he said.

Charmer, Homegirl said and didn't smile. She poured the drinks full, tho, handed one to Shadow, and patted the couch next to her.

He sat and his neck roll throbbed and he loved it.

Cheers, Homegirl said and held out her glass.

They cheersed and drank. Homegirl rubbed her boot a little more. Shadow remembered all the times he'd seen her running naked to the bathroom and wondered what the hell she wanted from him when he knew Punkboy did more than all right by her. He knew cos he heard them all night long, even with ear plugs; he knew cos he fell asleep dreaming of her shimmering cunt.

He dreamt it was shimmering, not glistening, so Homegirl was slightly off. Just slightly, tho. Not enough to really count.

He knew it wasn't sex she was after from him and that's all he could think of.

He knew it wasn't sex, but that's all and forever what he'd want from her. He couldn't let her know, tho. Not yet. He took a large gulp of his bourbon; his whole neck ached now and he was having trouble both looking at Homegirl and looking away.

The twinge in his neck had turned into a vise. The vise was squeezing, squeezing on both sides and he didn't want to look too much at Homegirl and give too much away, but the vise wouldn't let him look away.

He was in deep already; he'd have to find some way to get the fuck free. He knew how and he knew it was coming but he wanted to savor this thin veneer of civilization for a few moments more.

Like he could ever live a normal life.

Where's Punkboy?, she said.

He shrugged; he'd been avoiding Punkboy ever since Punkboy'd cornered him in the kitchen and demanded to know, was desperate to know where Homegirl was.

Shadow knew desperation. He could smell; he could taste it. Punkboy's desperation'd been somewhat threatening, so he'd told him what he knew rather than having to fight and maim Punkboy and have the cops involved and everything. Homegirl's desperation was not so threatening. He was swishing Homegirl's desperation in his mouth right now, it was fruity and deep and finished on a long note; he might be able to use this to his advantage.

He knew he could use it to his advantage.

What do you want?, he said.

Let me tell you a story, she said. She uncrossed and crossed her legs again. Her one thigh was so close to him; he could grab it in his big meaty hands, his broken knuckle hands, and pin her down if he wanted to. He thought about this as she took a sip of bourbon; he thought about this the whole time she told her story.

He only half-listened to her story.

She said, There are things I want.

There are things I want, too, Shadow said and licked his

whiskeyed lips.

Homegirl said, There are things I want and I will tell you why.

& Homegirl took a long pull on her highball glass and then launched into her story; her story was about someone doing her wrong just like he thought it would be and he was thinking about doing her wrong the whole time she was telling her been done wrong story. He knew her cunt would shimmer for his cock, even against her will.

She was talking about being tied up, and his neck was done throbbing and his neck was ready to move again.

Then she started talking about losing the baby; then she started talking about never being able to have a baby.

He remembered his pregnant fiancée being blown apart and he was full of glistening rage and he wanted to rage against everything; he was gonna rage against Homegirl's shimmering, glistening cunt whether she wanted it or not. He was gonna stick his cock in all the way up to her brains, past her brains and out to where his fiancée and child lay in a field of bits and pieces.

Or maybe it was someone else's pregnant fiancée and he'd blown her to bits.

Maybe there were many pregnant bitches and men fucking them and young boys with machine guns in their one remaining arm going around and cleaning up the mess afterwards.

Wombs exploding red and fetusy, maybe.

He couldn't remember and it didn't matter. It was probably all of the above cos the world was more than fucked up and people were way worse than animals and all that mattered was the rage that made him hard.

Shadow was a mercenary motherfucker, and he'd seen and done much much worse things than Richboy ever could even imagine. In his wildest fucking dreams.

He was gonna fuck Homegirl to pieces; she'd never see it coming. He took a long drink of his now watered down bourbon. The cold whiskey glinted on his glistening gums. He licked his lips again.

Shadow said, What's his name, again?, even tho Shadow knew his name and even knew where he'd just run off to. He leaned close like it was better to hear her with, but it was really so his one big hand could close around her thigh and his other big hand could open her up.

There was the sound of a key turning in the lock.

Lucky for Homegirl, Punkboy was home.

Shadow said, We'll continue this later.

He took his gums and his glass of bourbon and glistened off to his room.

TWENTY-EIGHT

When he saw Homegirl sitting alone on his couch, Punkboy was all like, What are you doing here?

Homegirl raised her glass. Drinking, she said.

Punkboy looked at her and was so glad she wasn't wearing that goddamned stained lingerie anymore. He didn't say anything, tho, just let his messenger bag fall to the floor from his hand. He was tired. Bonedogtired. He sat down next to Homegirl and she said, I got my job back, and then she handed him her drink. He held it up to cheers her and then finished it; he poured another, took a long gulp and handed it back to her.

He didn't want to fight and he didn't even know if he was still mad. If the anger had only been posturing, a way to propel himself away from that pathetic version of Homegirl that he never wanted to see again. The Homegirl with the bloodied merry widow and the vacant look and the sorrow. The Homegirl that didn't fight back; that acted like she deserved that fucked-up shit.

He wanted his feisty bitch back; he wanted his feisty bitch and he would wait.

She took a long swallow of bourbon from the glass and handed it back to him.

They were quiet on the couch.

Punkboy'd thought about finding out who leased the flat where he'd recovered Homegirl that night. What'd he do to those responsible and how far he'd go. He didn't own any weapons and he didn't want to, but he did know a bunch of beefy beer-bellied Miltown skaters and punks. They'd be down with beating the shit out of someone who done what'd been done to Homegirl.

His girl: Homegirl.

He didn't want to think about it right now, tho; he wanted to sit here in the dark quiet, on this couch, not have to talk, not have to do anything, and share bourbon from a highball glass with his girl.

He could tell Homegirl felt the same way; they sat there for hours, their bodies touching slightly, their hands brushing each other's as they passed the glass back and forth. Then they went to bed to sleep in each other's arms.

& it was good & quiet & the darkness was a good, quiet darkness. The darkness was a tamed dog curled sleeping at their feet; the darkness did not bark or growl or thrash about or lunge at them, for once.

TWENTY-NINE

Homegirl went to class that night.

Homegirl went to class; she made herself do it.

Homegirl hadn't been to class in three weeks and was afraid spitty prof'd say some things cos those were her three absences and he might use the whole absence thing as a way to get near her sex things.

Homegirl went to class and she was afraid Richboy'd show.

Homegirl went to class and she didn't have a gun in her purse or a knife in her boot or mace in her bra or poison in her ring or arrows in her cooch or anything; she came unarmed and that's why she was afraid.

She sat down in her usual space and felt like everyone knew and everyone was staring and judging and everyone was like, Yeah, slut or, Duh, you deserved it, or, Why didn't you do something?

Actually they were all just trying to figure out why both Richboy and she hadn't been to class in three weeks and then why tonight she'd come in without Richboy right behind her cos the two of them had been meeting up outside class ever since the start of the second class and all their classmates, even the older oblivious ones knew there was something going on, even the prof knew and the prof was pissed cos he wanted to take a bite out of Homegirl's juicy ass, he wanted to see her up on his desk with her ass cheeks spread, but diplomaed and safe intelligentsia can never compete with young and hot and maudlin.

Class started.

The prof said, Has anyone seen Richboy?

No one answered.

The prof said, Homegirl, have you seen Richboy?

The whole class was really staring at her now. She just shook her head no. Her face was burning burning almost as much as her hate and she was glad she hadn't brought a gun cos she was feeling a huge fucking bunch of rage, a giant inordinate anger at this spitty little prof and his stupid question.

He's supposed to turn a story in for workshop tonight, the prof said.

The rest of the class nodded and looked at each other and thought, as a collective, that would be just the kind of thing hot, young, and maudlin would do, skip out on his own story.

That's when Richboy walked in with copies of his story in his hands. Mimeographs no less. The librarian lady clapped her hands together excitedly. The prof didn't say anything snarky. Homegirl burned and burned. She was so hot and burning the old woman on her left thought, feeling waves of heat again, that she might be having a hotflash flashback or something and thought about leaving the classroom to cool down. Homegirl was so hot and burning, Richboy knew better than to sit next to her. He sat down next to the prof.

And the prof was happy, and the prof handed out Richboy's untitled story.

And this is Richboy's story.

And this is the story that made the prof, when he read it that night, say, hmmm, with a scrunched-up orgasm face.

And this is the story that made Homegirl burn so bright she glowed and kept Punkboy up that night all night.

& this is the story that Shadow knew was coming, that Shadow stopped mid-beat-off to recognize when he saw the fiery glow coming from under Punkboy's door and he knew it weren't no shimmering cunt giving off that too bright light.

And this is the story that Homegirl knew would be coming, and this is the story that welcomes a gun that asks for a knife that wants mace in the face that licks poison from her ring and plunges the arrow in itself:

There is a guy who follows me and writes everything I do and say and see and hear and think down. That is why I do these things that I do. I do the bad things and then I do the worse things but the guy doesn't say anything, he just writes. He doesn't go away and that is all I want. He just writes; he should be wearing a lab coat or he should have a diploma and he should be asking me questions, not just writing always writing.

He writes things like, *He thinks I should be wearing a lab coat or I should have a diploma.*

He writes things like, *Sometimes he thinks I'm a shrink and sometimes he thinks I'm a scientist and once when he was really drunk and laying on his back in the grass by the sidewalk with his dick out pissing and getting piss all over and thinking it was the funniest fucking thing ever, I showed up and I was Vaseline smeared fuzzynice so he thought I was God.*

He writes things like, *He will find a skinny girl and he will tell her her arms and legs are too bony and that they cut into him and he bleeds just looking at her and will you put on some weight, please, you're piercing my eyes.*

And things like, *He will find a chubby girl and tell her he is lost in her flesh. He will say he cannot find his way out and he will tell her she needs to get exit sign tatts and bright lights to point them out and that she needs to stop stuffing her fucking face.*

This is what I have to put up with; this is why I piss myself and laugh.

This is why, she, well, she, yes. You'll see.

I never thought she was fat, really, and I never wanted any babies. The two became conflated somehow and it had something to do with that guy always writing writing and when I looked at her up close I saw that her belly was made of babies and that her skin was little babies squirming under my hands and her blood was little babies doggy-paddling and laughing and sputtering and that the cries she cried out during our sex times were little babies getting out from her cavernous mouth, her black hole of a mouth, and they were crawling out onto my sheets and up onto my pillows and they wanted to get in my ears and play rattling drumming things in my head, they wanted to hiccup and poop and squish peas out their mouths in my head and I said, "I cannot have babies in my head, woman."

She started to cry and I was afraid the babies would come out her eyes. I turned her over roughly like I was going to take her from behind and set a palaver under her face. I set a paladin under her face. I set a pallor upon her. I set a platter on her.

I said, "Baby, don't cry. Don't cry, baby."

She wants to be my baby. She wants to crawl in my ear, too, and whisper things in my head. She wants to whisper sweet whispering birds and rabbits and beards and buggerboos and how am I supposed to hear her sweetsome crap over all her babies?

I said, "The babies will go to heaven." But she doesn't believe in it and I don't either and even the guy following me around who knows my thoughts because he once was a baby in my head doesn't believe in heaven either.

That's why he wasn't God when I was pissing and laughing and that's why I pissed on him, too.

Hell is so much easier and I would send her babies there just to show them if I could.

Her babies only slip out when I fuck her.

I will fuck her and fuck her and fuck her up against a wall and across my bed and on the toilet and in the shower and out in a dumpster and upside down from a wrecking ball and over Niagara Falls and in a lion's mouth and at the top of the Eiffel tower and in Houdini's water trap and I will fuck her hard and harder until she can't walk and she wants me to stop but she doesn't really and the babies will wriggle out her mouth and the thought of them will keep me hard.

The thought of killing them will keep me hard until they're all gone.

I will drown the babies in my cums, but that will make more babies and it will just never never fucking end, will it?

THIRTY

Homegirl read the story in Punkboy's bed; there was no other place she could have read it. She read while Punkboy picked out seeds and then packed a bowl. It felt normal; it felt domestic even.

Homegirl felt safe for a minute so she could read the story.

At the end of class, cos she was much farther from the classroom door than Richboy, Homegirl'd waited until almost everyone'd left to make an exit. She didn't want to run into him unprepared.

She didn't want to run into him without a weapon.

A real weapon.

She wished she owned a gun; she'd never wanted a gun before. She'd never understood the appeal. Now she thought them sexy metallic gleaming; now she wanted a little one she could strap into a garter and pull out on any fool that tried to mess with her.

She wanted to be a femme fatale + Mr. T.

I pity the fool...

She'd gotten out of the classroom without seeing him in the hall so she went the long way out the building in case he was smoking outside the other doors. She didn't know what she'd do if she saw him and she didn't want to know, yet.

She got to the parking lot and got in her car and felt safe, briefly.

Then she thought she heard his voice and saw two people

near the English building, talking and smoking.

She thought about driving up there. Driving fastfastfast, revving the engine now…

But she didn't want any witnesses, so she drove out of the parking lot and towards Punkboy's house and texted him at a stoplight cos she wasn't any good at driving & texting and Punkboy said he was at home and Punkboy said, Come over, and Punkboy said, Text me when you get here.

She did and Punkboy was already at the door even before she got up the stairs.

Punkboy held his door open for her & Homegirl wanted to say lots of things to Punkboy. Lots and lots of things that she'd never said to anyone else ever and because she'd never said any of these things she was feeling/thinking to anyone else, Homegirl didn't say them to Punkboy. Lots and lots of things that she'd been storing up for a long time and that Punkboy deserved to know and some of them even had something to do with him and some of these were deep things about Punkboy that she barely let herself know or think about, and she should have and part of her knew she should have and part of her really wanted to say all these things, even the downdeep things about Punkboy, and it was like the words were right there, like the cliché tip of the motherfucking tongue. She could feel the words in her mouth, she rolled them around like tobacco or like wine but she couldn't spit and she couldn't swish and she couldn't spit them out.

She did say, Hi. Then she walked past him into his hall and then into the living room. Punkboy followed her.

Punkboy said, Like a drink?

She said, Sure.

He said, Whatcha like?

Homegirl said, Whatever.

Punkboy went to the kitchen and came back with two whiskey manhattans. Whiskey manhattans were her fave. Homegirl thought, Does he even know that's my fave.

Then she thought, Probably.

Then she thought, When did I tell him?

Then she thought, I've been knowing this guy & his cock for over three years.

Then she thought, That is a long time.

Punkboy said, How was class?

And Homegirl still hadn't told him whose flat he'd found her at or how she knew that person, so Homegirl couldn't tell him really about class; all she could do was shrug and sip her manhattan and appreciate the fact that all the liquor in it, which it was made of except for the maraschino, was perfectly balanced.

They drank their highballs and then Punkboy got up and he extended his hand to Homegirl and he kinda kiddingly pulled her up and they went to his bedroom.

& they fucked.

Punkboy was afraid at first cos of the shit that went down and the lost baby & the infected uterus & the loss of the babymakings; he was afraid Homegirl'd reject his advances and/or slap him for putting the moves on her.

Homegirl was afraid cos she hadn't fucked anyone since Richboy and look where that'd got her and it was bad real bad and she never ever wanted to everever give anyone that kind of power over her. So she was kind of on edge as Punkboy moved his tongue over her body, over her breasts, down her stomach, into her valley, down into her clit and then into her asshole.

When he started licking her asshole, she knew she had nothing to fear from him and she let go.

& when he was done licking, she said, I want you in me.

They were both so happy she'd said that that they both came right away. There was no all night fuckfest and that's how Homegirl came to be reading that story on Punkboy's bed and that's how Punkboy came to be cleaning and smoking the gangas and that's how Shadow came to be beating off and then Homegirl finished the story and she was burning and she so wanted to be pyrokinetic and go all firestarter on Richboy's ass. She was burning and she couldn't stop.

She was burning burning and she kept everyone in the house awake all night as she lay there imagining different deaths for Richboy.

They were many and detailed, just like Dante's rings of Hell.

But she hadn't even gotten around to imagining his afterlife, yet.

Which would be worse: to go on forever tormented or to just stop?

THIRTY-ONE

Shadow'd been trolling in his hoopdie. Shadow hadn't been following Homegirl cos Punkboy almost never let her out of his sight lately. Like he knew something. Like he knew what Shadow's one big hand'd always wanted, always even before he even got near her cos that's how Shadow does and that's how Shadow rolls.

Punkboy has no real idea how Shadow rolls; Punkboy met Shadow as a fellow pot smoker. Punkboy'd known there was a darker, seedier side to him, but he'd only begun to realize the darkness and the seed Shadow'd come from.

Shadow was bored and Shadow was trolling, like I said.

Shadow was bored and whoever caught his interest I'd pray to some kind of deity for them if I weren't incredulous.

Shadow never thought he'd help Homegirl out; he didn't really care what Richboy'd done except for the fact that Richboy'd been there in her pussy and Punkboy'd been there in her pussy and probably a lot of other guys'd been there in her pussy and that's why she deserved what his hand wanted from her.

But, he was bored and creeping in his hoopdie and he knew where Richboy was hiding out.

Richboy was shacking up with his Craigslistwitch cos he didn't want to pay rent and she cooked him meals. Fucking Homegirl'd never offered to cook him shit. Craigslistwitch aka Roomy'd moved here and gotten a job and a place after that one night cos she had liked the fucking and she had liked the fright.

That one night where they'd tortured Homegirl and miscarried her and fucked was magical to her and she knew downdeep she'd never have another like it.

Unless she hooked up with a serial killer.

That's my thought, tho, not hers. & that answers my question of why some bitches go along with the crazy mens who kill women. & why some crazy bitches lure them in for their crazy mens to kill.

There are a few women serial killers, but only a few.

Oh yes, there Meta goes again. On some kind of weird soapboxy thing &/or trying to score with the chicks…

Shadow'd been shadowing Craigslistwitch and Richboy even before he'd had that convo with Homegirl on the couch. Shadow wasn't really interested in justice, but vengeance/violence gave him a motherfucking hard on and, like I said, he was bored.

Shadow was both bored and pissed; he was bored cos he couldn't get Homegirl alone so he could fuck her hard, fuck her brains out, put his big fat cock up in her and out her head like he wanted to, and pissed cos that story'd kept Homegirl up burning and kept him from coming cos she was burning and she wasn't fucking all night like she usually did.

The night after the night Homegirl burned bright, he parked his car outside Craigslistwitch's lower level flat and watched and surveyed. He'd been doing that for a couple of nights now, this watching surveying thing and so he found out that Craigslistwitch did not have a dog. He could get in and hide wherever he wanted to; he could get in and not hide; he could get in and partake of whatever liquor cabinet they had; he could get in and go through both of their underwear drawers and their computers, if he wanted to.

He got in and went straight for the liquor.

No one was home cos Craigslistwitch and Richboy were at that dive bar that Richboy liked and Richboy was pretending to like Craigslistwitch that way and Craigslistwitch was trying to pretend she didn't like Richboy that way too much.

Shadow made himself an old fashioned as he waited; he was almost impressed their cabinet had bitters.

Craigslistwitch and Richboy both drank Hamm's cos Richboy was still trying to convince everyone Hamm's was the next Pabst.

Shadow made himself another drink and found Craigslistwitch's porn and put it in the Hello Kitty TV/VCR and settled into Craigslistwitch's lime green uncomfortable modular couch. He definitely didn't mind watching chicks get fucked as he waited for his fucks to get back.

He especially appreciated the chicks fucking the other chicks with the strap ons and the dildos. The segment with the purple dildo and the white whipped cream and the pink asshole stretching stretching was especially nice.

He would be nice to Craigslistwitch just for that.

Well, nice in his way nice at least.

THIRTY-TWO

Homegirl'd been staying at Punkboy's house again, ever since she'd started pretending to be back to normal. Ever since she'd started, Punkboy'd seemed more protective of her. Much more protective than when she'd been sitting on her bed freaking out in the stained lingerie.

She didn't understand it.

Maybe he knew she was just pretending.

She thought she was doing a damn fine job tho.

What she didn't realize was that she was burning through the night. That she was keeping Punkboy up with her burning; that he sometimes woke up on the floor next to the bed cos it was too hot in his bed with her burning in it and he thought, how did I get here?

& while he was half asleep he knew the answer, even if he forgot it as soon as he crawled back into bed and slept until morning.

The answer stayed somewhere in his brain, under the layers of DIY and cannabis and PBR.

Homegirl felt like he hardly ever let her out of his sight now; he even followed her to the bathroom and not to watch her shit and get turned on. He made her breakfast and lunch and even dinner; he offered to walk her to work and when she said, no, I'm driving there, he said, let me drive.

She said, You don't have a license.

He said, Who cares?

She said, You don't drive.

He said, I do now.

Then they both shut up cos neither of them really wanted to talk about why he could drive now.

So when Punkboy left for work that night, Homegirl was überhappy or at least übersomething. Homegirl was happy or something cos somehow she had the shift off and now she could do what she'd been planning to do all while pretending to be back to normal. She'd been wanting to do this planning thing for a while, but she and Punkboy seemed to be working a lot of the same shifts; little did she know Punkboy'd bribed their cafe manager with black market xanex and valium to schedule Homegirl and him together almost always.

For this night someone else had bribed the manager with an origami eighth of cheap cocaine.

It hadn't been Homegirl tho she'd been waiting and waiting for this night or moment or opportunity or whatever. Waiting through vegan eggs benedict and wading through couple cuddling time on his bed and waiting through movie time on the couch and waiting through six packs of PBR tallboys and through vegetable primavera and everything that just a while ago she woulda been so happy to sit and wait for.

All the shit she'd been waiting for and wanted a while ago she didn't give a fuck about. Even the vegan eggs benedict.

Really, Homegirl, really. Where you ever gonna find another guy that makes that shit? That cares enough to pervert the tastiness that is the Benedicts.

But Homegirl was on a mission.

She was gonna find Richboy.

She knew where to find Richboy.

Not cos of Shadow or anything. & not cos she was a super spy. But cos Roomy was friends with Richboy on Facebook and Roomy'd sent out invites for her housewarming party over Facebook and she hadn't made the party private.

Homegirl'd missed the party.

Homegirl'd missed the party on purpose.

Homegirl wanted to get the two of them alone; she wanted to make them suffer.

It was almost all she thought about. Even when she was being fed by Punkboy, being held by Punkboy, being licked and even fucked by Punkboy, she was thinking about making them hurt; what Richboy's deepdeep voice would sound like when he was really in pain from her slamming his nuts with her pocket Glock or maybe even blowing them off with it – she did buy a gun, yes she did – and what Roomy's voice would sound like when Homegirl twisted her nips with burning clamps or some shit.

She was not knowing Roomy's real identity as a Craiglistwitch yet.

If she knew, the burning would burn all the time and Punkboy's house probably woulda went up in flames before this.

Punkboy left for work; Homegirl was still laying in his bed. He'd kissed her good-bye and Homegirl thought, This may be the last time you see me.

She didn't say it, tho.

She got up and got dressed and got into her car and drove to the dive bar she and Punkboy liked to hang out at. It was her way of saying good-bye to Punkboy.

It was 6 o'clock at night when she got there. She parked on a side street and walked past the peeling white sides to the front; she opened the door and it seemed like time stopped.

Everyone in the bar stopped.

Everyone in the bar was a white man and they all stopped.

Everyone in the bar was a white man who hadn't been laid or hadn't been laid properly in a while and they all stopped and stared at Homegirl as she walked in.

Everyone in the bar was a white man and older than Homegirl and some of them actually seemed to be drooling into their cheap taps as she walked up to the bar.

I forgot to tell you Homegirl'd dressed for battle. I forgot to tell you Homegirl'd dressed to throw down. I forgot to tell you Homegirl'd put on a plaid schoolgirl mini and knee high boots and a tight tank and she'd straightened her bangs and her hair obsessively and she'd liquid eyelinered her eyes all 60s cat eyes and she'd liplined her lips all red and filled in the lines with red red lipstick.

She went up to the bar and said, Who's gonna buy me a drink?

She went up to the bar and said, Who gots a cigarette?

She got a drink and a cigarette and a light and she nodded at the white man who gave these things to her and he just kind of disappeared. There was a power in her nod, a power to disappear. She shoulda used that nod on Richboy when he'd first sat down next to her.

She will remember the nod; she will use the nod if another Richboy ever tries to enter her life.

The white men all watched her as she sat and drank and smoked at the bar; Homegirl didn't pretend to be doing anything else, didn't pretend to be texting or watching TV or waiting on anybody. She was drinking a drink and smoking a smoke and for once wasn't anxious that she was alone.

She pushed her highball glass forward for another. The bartender refilled her drink and pointed at a man at the end of the bar and said, He's got this one.

Homegirl nodded at that man, too, and poof he was gone.

I watched, knowing better than to buy Miss Homegirl a drinky-drink cos this was not magic and it was not magical realism; I didn't know what the fuck it was and where the mens were going. I had no control over it at all.

What would happen if she disappeared me? Me, Meta? Would she be stuck forever at the bar, drinking and smoking but not getting drunk or even reaching a nicotine rush? Would the vague white men keep buying those drinks and getting disappeared? Were there a finite number of vague white men and would they stop showing up and buying her drinks? Or were they infinite, these vague white men? They'd keep coming up to the bar and talking to the bartender and Homegirl'd get her drink on and on and on and on, as long as she didn't nod in that nodding way at the bartender.

I didn't want to find out what would happen if she disappeared me, so I sat in a darkened corner of the bar, out of the range of Homegirl's nod.

Just to show us all, tho, she took a sip of her drink and nodded at a guy for the hell of it and he was gone.

Then she took out that black moleskine and settled down

to write.

This is what she wrote:

That baby is a girl baby and that baby is always watched. That baby feels the watchful eyes before that baby knows what eyes are. That baby feels eyes watching before that baby knows what that baby is. That baby is dressed in pink but that baby does not know pink or clothes and only knows that white shapes come and go and that the world moves and that the world is still and that when that baby opens that mouth there is a sound like.

That baby does not have words and that baby can barely see. But that baby knows the feeling of watching eyes.

The watching eyes do not go away even when the words come.

Even when some words come, that baby is still dressed in pink and the eyes that watch still watch.

More eyes watch that baby that is dressed in pink. That baby with words starts to think maybe the pink is what brings the eyes that watch. That baby hides in corners and takes off its clothes when it does not feel the eyes watching. That baby runs naked through rooms until the eyes that watch become tongues that click and hands that hit.

That baby is a bad baby.

That baby likes to run outside when it rains.

That baby likes to put on cowboy boots first then run outside when it rains.

That baby likes to leave its pink dress on the porch and run through the rain pink naked in pink cowboy boots. That baby feels the rain on that baby's pink skin and it is a feeling like.

The mouths make many sounds over that baby and the eyes make many looks and that baby doesn't know all the words but that baby knows the feeling of the words and knows that the eyes will always be watching and the mouths will always be moving and there is no way to get away from the moving talking watching eye-mouths and that the rain can only keep them at bay for so long. For so long that baby kicks puddles up with pink cowboy boots. That baby puddles with the boots and the rain and knows someday that that baby will splash-kick the watching eyes and nod nod nodding make them all disappear.

Homegirl ripped out the empty pages of the moleskine and left them on the bar and then closed the book. She wouldn't write in this one ever again.

Then she pushed her glass forward for one more drink and after getting the drink, nodded good-bye and left.

THIRTY-THREE

Homegirl left the dive bar after having three drinks; she was feeling a little tipsy cos she hadn't really eaten that day, but she knew she could aim her pocket Glock if she had to and that's all she cared about. She planned on going up to Roomy's flat, knocking on the door and being let in.

It didn't go down like that, of course.

She left the dive bar without even having to nod at any white man in her way; they saw her get off her bar stool and they all scattered. She left the bar and walked to her car alone. She only had to drive a little ways.

She parked and turned off the car and grabbed the Glock out of her glove compartment and put it in her boot. It was a tiny woman's Glock and she didn't feel stupid or like a stereotype or a weakling cos even if it was small the shit would still shoot and kill if she needed it to.

When she got to the door of the flat there was no knock knocking cos when she got to the lower door of the upper flat it was very slightly ajar and she slipped in.

In the vestibule she closed the door behind her and grabbed her tiny Glock from her boot. She walked up the stairs quietly cos she didn't know why the door was ajar. Maybe Roomy and Richboy were expecting her; maybe they set all this shit up.

Like they set her up the last time.

She got to the top of the stairs and their flat door and of

course she paused, Glock in hand. What did you expect? She paused for a sec and then pushed the door softly.

It was unlocked and opened at her push.

She thought, Okay.

She thought, Shit.

She thought, Wtf is going down here? And she walked through the doorway with her gun ready.

There was no one there, but there were weird sounds coming from somewhere. Weird muffled sounds that kinda sounded like the sounds she'd imagined Richboy would make when she shot him in the balls with her Glock except he'd make these sounds if she also gagged him first, and she'd never planned on gagging him cos she wanted to hear all his suffering.

She wanted his suffering to be the song she never forgot.

But these sounds were the Glock shot nuts sounds she'd expected from Richboy + gag and what the fuck was going on?

She walked into the first room from the flat's door and it seemed to be a dining room and it seemed like the dining room was an office cos the dining room table had a big computer on it. & all the lights were on.

Homegirl couldn't hide in any shadows of shadows. It was all too bright. Even the computer was on.

It was all too bright and Homegirl was feeling like she should get the fuck out of there while she could, but she was curious and stubborn and she'd brought a gun. She walked into what was the kitchen and on the counter there was a half drunken drink and she sniffed it and then she drank it. It tasted like whiskey, bourbon really, and 7up and bitters, and Homegirl was for a minute afraid and she gripped her gun more tightly with one hand and raised the drink to her mouth again with the other.

Just as she finished the drink she heard a muffled scream and more muffled nut pain. There were two people in pain now, and Homegirl thought she knew who they were.

But, who was doing her dirty work?

Did Punkboy really go to work or was that a lie?

Was Punkboy torturing Roomy and Richboy for her?

Was Punkboy torturing them for the fetus?

Homegirl'd seen Punkboy's face when she'd come back from the examining room at Planned Parenthood; she saw his face and she'd catalogued it in her brain for later cos she could only process the fucked-upness of her Fallopians at that time. She'd catalouged it and it came up when she was dreaming and even when she was reading and subconsciously she knew what that face looked like and what it meant and it meant pain and suffering and it was part of the reason why she burned and burned so bright at night.

THIRTY-FOUR

Pocket glock in hand, Homegirl walked towards what she thought would be a bedroom. The door, like the flat door, was slightly ajar. Homegirl took a deep breath cos she didn't know what else to do besides the cliché at this moment.

What do you do with a gun in your hand about to burst into some fucked up shit?

Of course, she pushed the door open with her glock and of course, she maneuvered her way in so the glock was always in front of her. And of course, she almost fell onto the torturer and his victims. But she didn't just. She stopped short with her glock pointing out and sighed once more.

Which is not cliché and you should never sigh in front of your enemy, I think. Well, I really don't know either. Maybe sighing as a sign of relaxation would get into the enemy mind, would unnerve the enemy maybe.

Homegirl stopped short and she saw a big bald guy with neck rolls with a curved fancy knife and she was like, Shadow. Then she saw a guy tied up in the bed and she was like, Richboy. Then she saw a woman tied up in a chair and she was like, Roomy. Shadow, seeing Richboy and Roomy's eyes going wider, turned around to face her; another cliché again, but all Shadow knows is cliché. Shadow's been fucked by the world since he was a pre-teen; he finds solace in its clichés cos at least with clichés he knows what's coming.

Homegirl stuck her Glock out in front of her more; she

waved it a little at all three. Richboy had a gag in his mouth, as did Roomy.

Shadow said, Hi.

She said, Hi.

I was still clean.

Richboy mumbled something through his gag; he was in his jockeys and his chest was bleeding. Roomy didn't try to mumble anything; she was still dressed. Shadow didn't say anything else, just held his knife out a bit and stared at Homegirl and her gun.

So, Homegirl said.

So, Shadow said. He believed in the cliché that repeating people's words put them at ease somehow.

So, Homegirl said, which didn't help Shadow out at all.

Shadow wasn't that worried, even tho Homegirl had a gun. He felt like he could take her if he had to. He didn't want to right now, as he'd been enjoying fucking with these two hipster fucks. Shadow hated people who pretended to be apathetic or nihilistic for no good reason than it was cool. Shadow would give them the reasons to be nihilistic; Shadow would give them reasons not to care beyond a doofus posturing.

Shadow'd been there and look at Shadow now. Shadow was nihilistic apathy.

Shadow enjoyed the knife and the blood and fear too much.

Is this what you really want to be, hipster fucks?

Homegirl stood there with her gun; she didn't know how to proceed, either. Richboy tried to sit up, like Homegirl would help him even. Roomy knew to sit back and wait, not cos she was a witch, but because she had probably the most common sense at this point.

Shadow finally said, So. Homegirl.

Homegirl said, Yeah.

Shadow said, Yeah. And tried to move towards her.

Homegirl waved her gun; it was a cliché and it worked, Shadow stopped moving.

It was a small bedroom with the four-poster bed by the wall with Richboy tied down on it on top of the Calvin Klein bedding and then Roomy tied to an ergonomic orange desk chair next to it with a blonde Ikea ergonomic workdesk behind her and Shadow's bulk in front of her and Homegirl with a glock in front of him.

What are you doing here?, Homegirl said.

Then she said, Don't ask me what I'm doing here; I'm on to you.

Shadow grimaced and felt the neck tingling thing and immediately got a hard on. Cleaning up after you, is what he said.

Huh?, Homegirl said.

Cleaning up for you, Shadow said again.

Come again?, Homegirl said and waved the glock some more. She was not playing dumb; she wanted Shadow to explain himself and what he was doing here torturing the only two people in the whole world Homegirl'd ever wanted to torture herself.

You told me what they did, Shadow said.

Did you know she was a witch?, Shadow said and then cuffed Roomy's head.

Oy, Homegirl said. She didn't know what else to say; she waved her glock some more.

Bitch met asshole through Craig's List, Shadow said.

Which one's bitch and which one's asshole?, Homegirl said.

Shadow smiled.

Richboy strained at his bindings; Roomy bit at her gag. Homegirl laughed cos she could and none of this was funny. None of it.

Let him talk, Homegirl said and waved her glock at the bleeding Richboy.

What about her?, Shadow said.

No, Homegirl said.

That's not very feminist of you, Shadow said.

What the fuck does that even mean? Let dude speak, Homegirl said.

Let him sit up, too, Homegirl said.

Shadow looked at her like what the fuck but Homegirl just stood there in her schoolgirl mini with her gun.

Homegirl wanted Richboy to feel some kind of hope for a second.

Homegirl wanted Richboy to feel some sort of hope before she killed him.

THIRTY-FIVE

This is the chapter where Punkboy saves them all.

This is the chapter where Punkboy shows up at the house. Surprise! & saves Homegirl from killing Richboy.

This is the chapter where surprise! Punkboy shows up and saves Homegirl from murdering a worthless dick and then declares his love for her.

This is the chapter – surprise! Punkboy appears, saves Homegirl, declares love, and asks her to marry him in front of Shadow's tied up victims and Shadow. Not until after Punkboy's sneak attack has rendered Shadow unconscious, of course.

Shadow looks like a bear rug on the bedroom floor.

A little bit of blood trickles from his forehead and he kinda snores.

Homegirl goes all, Yes yes! & Punkboy and she start making out wildly and fall onto the bear rug that is unconscious Shadow & that is not sexy so they help each other up and they untie Craigslistwitch and Richboy cos they don't care about them anymore cos they're in love and going to get married and they never have to worry about having the babies which would kill the love and the sexing.

This is the chapter where everything comes together nicely.

This is the chapter where Roomy aka Craigslistwitch and Richboy decide to make a go of it, seeing Punkboy & Homegirl's happiness.

This is the chapter where Shadow wakes up alone on the floor and has an epiphany, of course.

This is the chapter.

Not.

THIRTY-SIX

These are the reasons Homegirl had to kill Richboy: her ovaries, her hatred, her pain, her torture, his privilege, his idiocy, his cruelty, his charm. These are not reasons, but these are factors: the darkness, all the times she's been dumped cos even tho she's not a man-hater that shit still hurts & resonates, Roomy aka Craigslistwitch, the fact that he can just drop her for another like that, and that there'll always be another and another and they'll have funkier bangs and be thinner and younger even as he gets older and dumber and crueler and puffier.

These are the reasons Homegirl had to not kill Richboy: she didn't know if she was up for the judgment and condemnation of the whole nation or at least the city; she could barely stand her parents' suburban neighbors' glances cos she knew they was always thinking what a slut or what the hell's that one doing with her life and she couldn't even stand her boyfriends' judgy looks sometimes when they'd surprised her at her house and her room had clothes strewn all over and the toilet looked like a frat boy's. Everyone would be judge judging if she killed the fucker; everyone would be looking and thinking things and making shit up and thinking more things and not in the way she'd want.

Sometimes she wanted to move away from people and this was without even having killed someone. Sometimes when her neighbors stopped her on her way to her hatchback and started yakking at her all she could think about was what they were thinking and what they were thinking was judgy of how she was food service sexing it up single woman.

Add murderer to that, yeah.

Add murderer to that & they'd all be like, yeah. That's about right. Bitch has no morals.

& bitch has a lot of morals but she hides them and they're her own morals and no one else's and they might allow murder.

Notice how Punkboy didn't come up as any of the reasons, pro or con?

I killed someone once, but I only wrote it that way. I don't know what Homegirl's gonna do. This may be the crossroads I promised you. This may be a crossroads or some crap like that.

THIRTY-SEVEN

Punkboy was at work in the kitchen. He was back there alone and he was stoned and he was slammed, but he was slamming the shit out as fast as the tickets were snapped up. He was slapping mayo on the subs with the thick mayo wand and thinking about Homegirl's ass as he slapped; he was throwing the meat down and thinking about throwing his meat down; he was cheesing the top of the sandwiches and imagining pulling out and creaming all over Homegirl's back; he was sticking those sandwiches in the salamander and thinking about sticking his dick in various Homegirly orifices…

You get the picture of what gets Punkboy through a late night dinner rush.

I Against I by Bad Brains was playing and Punkboy felt young and hard and able even tho the album'd come out when he was a preteen and following his meathead of a bro to Judas Priest concerts instead of being himself and listening to punk rock.

So Punkboy was in a sandwich making sex thinkings zone and he was banging those sandwiches and salads out and he was also keeping track of what they'd need to prep tomorrow morning cos he had to leave a note at the end of his shift for the openers and he was also keeping track of images of Homegirl's perfect pink nipples and her round white buttocks in his mind when 'Sacred Love' came on.

Egyptiantatts turned it up cos Egyptiantatts was working counter and he was high high high on coke and he didn't care if the East Side punk-boho poseurs and teensters and scenesters got annoyed and called the office cos the music was too loud.

Which happened at least once a month and then their boss came in and called a work meeting and gave them beer and bitched at them and made them feel like shit while he got them drunk. The other owner sometimes came and sometimes didn't; she didn't care as much about customer complaints cos she knew the suckers'd still keep on coming in and that's all she cared about. That's all dude cared about, too, really, but he liked to pretend he cared about his customers as people. All the workers knew he was full of shit so they only half felt like shit while they got drunk as he yelled at them about the music volume and choice and anything else people'd complained about. A lot of times it was also their attitudes.

Homegirl'd been called "uppity" by a few people.

Punkboy'd been called "surly."

Casualty'd been called "catatonic."

Egyptiantatts'd also been called "uppity"; he'd been called "assholish," too.

The worst Engagedguy'd been called was quiet; maybe cos he was short and so didn't come off as cocky or maybe he was nice and just didn't like Homegirl or maybe he was just quiet and that's why he'd never talked to Homegirl.

I won't list all the other workers and their complained about attitudes cos I haven't even introduced you to them and there's a bunch of café bitches that would love to steal the spotlight from Homegirl and even Punkboy. Or they'd like to steal Punkboy from Homegirl.

Fucking café bitches, according to Homegirl.

Punkboy was thinking the sex food service prepping sandwiches things and he was also starting to think about leaving Homegirl alone tonight. For the first time since…

He didn't want to think about that and so he imagined her on his bed and she was naked and waiting for him and he was telling her come over and bend over but when she did she was wearing that bloodied merry widow and she was crying.

He hoped that she was okay.

He tried to imgine her again, face down on his bed, ass hanging off and he was behind her with hard cock in hand and she was naked and he was gonna put it in her wet cunt and then just like that she was on her knees on her bed in that fucking bloody merry widow again.

He sliced open a batard and tried not to think anything.

It worked for a sec or two.

Punkboy was in the middle of slapping mayo on a batard when 'Sacred Love' came on and then he was slapping more mayo on the batard as Egyptiantatts turned it up and he was slapping even more mayo on it as the refrain came on and when the song was over, Punkboy realized he'd just slathered the batard in mayo for the whole 3 minutes and 40 seconds of the song and he hadn't once thought of slapping Homegirl's ass the whole time. And sandwiches were starting to burn in the salamander.

Something was wrong.

Something was wrong with Homegirl.

He threw the mayo wand in the mayo tin on the prep table; he unknotted his white apron and let it fall to the floor; he yelled, Egyptiantatts, sorry, dude, I'm outie, and then he left through the back door.

The back door led into an alley where they all smoked the gangas like I said. The back door was also the door the dude owner took you to when he fired you on the spot. The alley was tagged all over in taggy scribbles by the WR Crew and Festick JC, who happened to be a smoking buddy of Casualty.

Casualty had many smoking buddies, of course.

Punkboy went out through the alley to the side of the café where his fixie was chained up. He unlocked it and hopped on it and he went looking for Homegirl. He was gonna bike around his neighborhood until he saw her car. He was gonna start with the house where he found her that one night and he was gonna hope the whole time he was biking around that she was safe in his bed waiting for him to come home.

Punkboy'd never had this feeling before of something terribly wrong and he'd never left work before the end of his shift even when he'd sliced his finger so bad he had a flap of skin just flapflapping and gushing blood and he'd had to cook with it gauzed and three surgical gloves on his injured hand. Then he'd gone for stitches, after he'd finished the orders and wiped the kitchen spotless.

So, he knew deepdown Homegirl wasn't in his bed and he knew he'd have to find her soon.

THIRTY-EIGHT

You and I know where Homegirl is, at Roomy's house with a gun. Shadow's just ungagged Richboy and loosened his restraints so he can sit up. Richboy's sitting up, shirtless and bleeding and even whiter than Homegirl's ever seen him. & dude's pretty fucking white cos the only sunshine he ever sees is when he stumbles from various girls' places early in the morning to escape the afterfuck wake-up/awkward greeting or when he stumbles from various drug dens after snorting or smoking for hours on end. Richboy doesn't shoot up cos he won't share needles.

Richboy doesn't like to share and Richboy doesn't like the sun cos he likes to walk the streets at night and smoke cigarettes and sweating in the sun's just not cool. It's about as cool as a brontosaurus drinking a martini tattoo on your neck.

Homegirl's got her gun trained on Shadow; Shadow's hovering near Richboy with a knife; Richboy's trying to think up a way to talk his way out of this; Roomy's just watching it all with her big blue eyes like a small child or like she's had no part in this and is incredulous she's even here at all.

Let me go, Richboy says, and I'll give you whatever you want.

Shadow scratches his cheek with the dull edge of his knife. Shadow says, Like what?

Richboy says, Money.

Shadow shakes his head.

Richboy says, Drugs.

Shadow shakes his head.

Richboy says, Girls.

Shadow says, I gots two right here with me.

Homegirl says, You don't have me. She waves her gun; she's trying not to shake. Why'd she ever fuck with Shadow? Dude creeps her out always and forever hardcore.

Shadow says, You're not gonna shoot me.

Shadow says, You want my big cock.

Shadow says, You want it up you so far it goes out your nose. It goes out your forehead and your eyeballs spray my jism. Shadow licks his lips. Yum.

Homegirl says, You are one sick fuck.

Richboy says, You can have her. I'm done with her. Richboy's decided Shadow's gonna win this one, gun or no gun.

Homegirl says, Fuck you.

Shadow says, Fuck you.

They say it at the same time; they look at each other. Homegirl spits on the floor. Homegirl never spits.

Shadow says, Where'd you get that little gun?

Homegirl says, What's it to ya?

Neither of them are paying attention to Roomy aka Craigslistwitch and the bitch's not only a witch but she's moonlighted as a magician's assistant, among many other very odd roles like watching porn for scientific research, a stunt girl, an Alaskan canner, etc. She's somehow managing to contort her body and the ropes to free herself. She's totally free, but she's gonna wait for the best moment to attack or run. She doesn't really have a plan, but she wants to protect what's hers and she's thinking Richboy's hers, especially if he's tied up.

Shadow says, Cos I might know something you don't. He's no longer hovering near Richboy. In fact, he's gotten closer to Homegirl somehow without any of the others even noticing him moving.

Why do you think he's called Shadow?

& Homegirl's called Homegirl cos she's always and forever looking for that home and always and forever resisting that urge to find home. She thinks love can be a home. She runs from the love that can be a home straight to the guys who want to knock that home on its ass, that want to raze every wall and kick in every door and break every tooth in that home. Guys like Richboy.

She's a modern day fucking Dorothy from Oz and instead of ruby slippers, bitch has a gun. & instead of the lion, the woodsman, and the scarecrow, she's gots her brains, her looks, and her cunt.

There's a wicked witch, too, and her name is Roomy.

Homegirl says, What do you know? & backs up a little from Shadow; she only backs up a little, tho, cos she doesn't want to corner herself against a wall. She's not quite sure where she's situated now. She feels a little dizzy and sick and is fighting the urge to run at the moment. Homegirl's telling herself she'll come out of this all right; she's gots the gun.

But that little sliver of doubt is all Shadow needs. He'll insinuate himself into that sliver and work that sliver until that sliver opens up a big fucking hole in her head. Homegirl's not even debating killing Richboy now. She's almost forgotten he exists. & he's being cannily quiet cos he wants to see how all this shit will play out.

Shadow says, Maybe you got that gun from a friend of mine. Maybe that gun don't work right.

Shadow talks cliché thugspeak in thuglife situations. Shadow is a consummate performer above all else in thuglife situations. It is his calling, his virtuosity.

Shadow smiles and takes a step closer.

Shadow says, Have you tried it out yet?

Homegirl and Shadow both look at her hand holding the gun. Homegirl doesn't know what to do. If she squeezes the trigger and nothing happens, she's fucked. If she squeezes and misses, she's fucked. If she squeezes and hits, maybe she'll be all right.

She could squeeze and hit and run.

The two are so intent on their game of gun chicken or whatever that neither of them notice Roomy lunging herself from her chair and sliding under the 4 poster bed. Neither of them know Roomy's got a gun under there; her mama was a Bible nut and her brothers were gun nuts and she'd said good-bye to the Bible a long time ago and her going away present from her bros was a gun.

It was one of the only things that ever made her feel loved.

She rolls back out with a S&W M&P 357 handgun and jumps up.

THIRTY-NINE

Veins are sticking out in three white hands – two gripping guns and one with a knife. Shadow's neck tingles have taken over his whole body and he hasn't felt this alive in a long long time. He will thank Craigslistwitch and/or Homegirl immensely for this.

I don't have to tell you how he wants to thank them.

The only thing Shadow loves more than violence is sex with violence. And maybe a touch of death.

Others', of course.

Homegirl's wishing she'd brought her little baby gun to the workshop and killed Richboy then, if she ever even was gonna do it. Homegirl's wishing she could just get the fuck out of here. She's wishing she'd never met any of these people she's stuck in this room and doesn't want to die with. She's afraid if she dies in this room with these people she'll be stuck in this room with them forever. Like Sartre's *No Exit*. Except this hell'll have rape and threeway rape and dildo rape and ear rape and skull rape and weird Tim Burton claymation pieces coming off and being put back together wrong rape and Richboy and Roomy getting it on over and over again as Shadow rapes her over and over out through her eyeballs and then her eyeballs are in her armpits and then they're in her anus and then they're on top of Shadow's head and then they're on the head of his penis as he rapes her nostrils and don't forget the guns and it won't be just the talky talking.

Even tho listening to them talky talking would be hell enough, she supposes.

Homegirl's wishing this were a bar and she could just nod them all away. Homegirl's wishing her new nodding powers extended beyond the bar and beyond old skeezers.

Homegirl's wishing for a deus ex machina.

If I had those powers, I could provide her one.

If I had those powers, I would have made her love me a long time ago and none of this shit would've gone down and there'd be no need for that deus ex machina in the first place. My powers seem to be limited, most def.

Homegirl and Craigslistwitch and Shadow are all looking at each other. Homegirl and Craigslistwitch are pointing their guns. It is uncomfortable; it is tense; it is awkward silence times 1,000.

Richboy breaks the silence. Richboy says, Kill her. Just kill the bitch already.

Homegirl says, Shut up. She wants to scream it. She wants to shoot her load right into him. But she knows if she shoots him then down she goes.

Craigslistwitch says, Shut up yourself, bitch.

Craigslistwitch's big breasts are of course, heaving.

Shadow says, This is so hot. He kind of moans.

Craigslistwitch and Homegirl both train their guns on him.

It is a triangle. There is no hypoteneuse in sight. Homegirl's trying to figure out the distance between a and b so she can get the fuck out of there.

Craigslistwitch says, Hey, big guy. She waves her S&W at

him to say hi kind of.

Shadow says, Chicks with guns. Chicks with big titties and guns even better. He giggles. I swear to god, he giggles.

Big man, Craigslistwitch says. Let's make a deal.

Homegirl says, Fuck you, skankwhore. & spits at her. & misses.

You are one fucking lucky Homegirl, Craigslistwitch says. I woulda voodooed your ass with that.

I'm gonna voodoo you, babykiller.

Craigslistwitch just laughs and says, Big man. You give me him. She points to Richboy. And I'll give you her and we all walk out of here alive.

Homegirl spits and hits Craigslistwitch this time. Homegirl laughs.

Then things happen so fast.

Shadow somehow grabs Craigslistwitch's arm and the gun goes off in the ceiling and Homegirl's watching and this is her chance to run, she knows.

This is her chance.

Shadow and Craigslistwitch are still grappling; Richboy's still tied up. Homegirl turns towards the door and then she looks back.

Never look back, Homegirl, never look back.

Richboy's chest is bleeding and Richboy's cock is poking up through his jockeys and Richboy's mouth's sneersmiling and his eyes are hardraping and then Richboy's mouth is opening and Homegirl thinks of the kissing and the hair pulling and the Thanksgiving stuffed snatching and thinks of the highballs and the waiting and the withholding and the spanking and the babies spilling spilling and thinks of the screen door slamming and then she knows, just knows, his open mouth is gonna screen door creak open grating to Craigslistwitch and Shadow that she's escaping.

Homegirl shoots and runs.

Homegirl shooting somehow hits Richboy in the heart. And his chest bursts open and his heart bursts within and it is like a desert flower bursting through the sand after a rare rare rain or some beautiful ironic messed-up shit like that and Richboy's almost surprised that he really does have a heart and that he really can bleed to death and he smiles surprised and innocent almost that he feels some thing for a rare desert minute and his eyes are soft and shimmering like Homegirl's cunt according to Shadow and death says, I will take all of you in my mouth, and he's all taken in and oh yesyesyes and he bleeds and bleeds and bleeds through the bed through the floor through the lower flat's ceiling and it is in the shape of a heart.

I fucking kid you not. A bloody fucking heart.

A la Tess and Thomas Hardy.

A heart raining its rare blood down on the downstairs neighbor's spare bedroom bed.

FORTY

Punkboy pedals pedals.

Punkboy pedals over or around every obstacle I throw at him: that empty Natty Light twelve pack, the blue pit bull dragging a heavy metal chain behind him, the crackhead whose car's broken down and he needs money so he and his pregnant wife can move to Muskego where he's gots a job waiting, his ex – why not? – the one he cheated on with Homegirl cos he could cos he didn't love either one at the time, she's in the middle of some street and she's screaming at him even tho it's been over a year, his mom's on the street corner asking him why he hasn't called, doesn't he love her, will he be coming for Thanksgiving?, his meathead half-bro's throwing shit at him, frat boy paraphernalia like street signs and blow up dolls and polo shirts and crew cuts and mandals and a blind adherence to white man's authority and traditions.

My powers seem to be limited to making sure Punkboy doesn't win.

I throw some more shit in his way like a barhopper drunkenly leaving her car and almost hitting him with the door, but my heart's not tot in it.

I don't want Punkboy to win but I def don't want Shadow or Richboy to win either. I am screwed. I am lose lose. Why couldn't I be motherfucking omniscient? Huh? Why'd that vogue have to run its course so motherfucking soon?

His cell phone's ringing and he knows it's his boss and

he's probably fired and it's almost ten now and dark and he's pedaling and ringing up and down Riverwest streets looking for Homegirl, looking for her hatchback, avoiding all my crap and he seems to be on to me, he keeps looking over his shoulder like he's being watched or followed.

He zips through the streets and any other night he would revel in the zip; he would zip and revel and fly and pedal, free. But tonight, well, yeah. You know almost as much as me and Punkboy's only got a feeling but he's listening to this feeling.

He gets to Wright St. where there's a bar that used to be a cool punk bar with the best jukebox in all the Midwest, no shit, but it's not a cool bar anymore it's a shady crack/coke bar unlike the all right coke/dive bar he hangs out at.

He thinks he hears Homegirl.

He thinks he hears Homegirl and Bad Brains together.

Bad Brains' singing something about love and Homegirl's saying, Trigger gun. What do I do? If I miss...

Homegirl's saying, Help.

Homegirl's saying, Deus ex machina.

Punkboy's pedaling faster and saying, I'm coming.

Punkboy's saying, Deus what?

And if Punkboy'd been able to get through the Bronte sisters' books without his bowling pin shaped leisure suit wearing bulldyke of an English teacher ruining *Wuthering Heights* or *Jane Eyre*, this might have seemed familiar.

He might have said, I am coming: wait for me.

He might have said, more softly, Where are you?

But, yeah, he didn't.

Then he didn't hear anything more. Then he was just

pedaling again; pedaling and not even ringing anymore and it was dark and it was quiet and it was Riverwest.

FORTY-ONE

Homegirl has just killed someone.

Homegirl never in her life thought she'd kill someone. Sure, she'd hated and wished people dead on a superficial level but she'd never made it happen before.

Homegirl was so fucked.

Homegirl was running down the stairs, out the door, and onto the porch

Punkboy was cycling; Punkboy was still looking for Homegirl.

Homegirl wasn't looking for Punkboy. She was just looking for a way out. Homegirl was too pretty to go to jail and that wasn't a cliché.

She was too pretty to go and the other prisoners would eat her alive more than any hipster scene could ever dream of doing. The prison was full of sad fucks like Homegirl and sick fucks like Shadow.

That was the jail. A distilled fucked-upness of the world in a cage. Two chicks enter; one chick leaves.

Punkboy was a sad fuck like Homegirl and he was still pedaling pedaling through trashy alleys and Judas Priest memories.

Homegirl's at her car and then in her car and she's sitting in the driver's seat now and her hands are shaking but there's no blood on them not even a damned spot and Homegirl wouldn't appreciate the irony at this moment; she'd tell me to

173

get fucked, I know.

Homegirl's shaking & she doesn't know what to do.

Homegirl's thinking she should split town.

Homegirl's wondering if she should even say good-bye to Punkboy.

Homegirl's thinking she needs a drink.

Homegirl's forgetting all about Shadow.

Homegirl needs to be thinking about Shadow.

As should all of us, locked in our cages.

You're saying, We get it, Meta. We get it. But, that's just what you say. You don't really get it. No one does. No one really gets it until we fucking die. & you're saying, now now, you're saying, oh Meta, you & your existential bullshit; you're just unhappies cos the woman you love thought she loved someone else and then she killed him so you should actually be happy she didn't love you cos you'd probably be in the ground.

Or burning in a bed by now.

& what about Punkboy?

FORTY-TWO

Homegirl didn't know what to do or where to go so she drove home.

With gun in her one hand, she steered her car with the other and made it home still shaking.

Casualty and Artfag were on the couch smoking the big bong when Homegirl rushed in. Homegirl'd forgotten to hide her gun; it was still in her hand.

She closed the big door with her glock and Casualty and Artfag saw it.

Whoa, said Casualty.

Is that real?, said Artfag.

Homegirl ignored them and ran into her bedroom. She had the only bedroom in the front of the house, with the window opening conveniently onto the front porch. Now this convenience seemed like a liability. Anyone could almost walk right in.

Shadow could almost walk right in; Shadow most probably knew where she lived. But, like I said, Homegirl wasn't thinking about Shadow.

Shadow was a creeping creeper and most def knew where she lived. But, Homegirl wasn't worried about him.

Homegirl was worried about herself. & what she'd done.

& a small part of her was worried about Punkboy. & a larger part of her was worried Punkboy would come find her.

But not Shadow. & I am a lot worried about him and I just

want to shake her.

& Casualty and Artfag were a lot stoned and a little worried. Not about Shadow either cos they didn't know Shadow or if they'd ever encountered Shadow, which was likely cos he hung around the periphery of all scenes, at the corner of all scenes, scoping out the weak females who drank too much and he could fuck and the weak males who drank too much and he could fuck over cos Shadow was tot heteronormative and played by gender's rules, they didn't remember, but, they knew that Homegirl'd been through some shit recently; they could tell cos she was forever wearing that merry widow and it wasn't like Homegirl to prance around the house in dishabille but she hadn't been prancing in the merry widow and that merry widow was the saddest negligee they'd ever seen – dirty, beat up, bloodied. It'd gotten to be so bad, the lanky Homegirl slouching to the bathroom in that sad scuffed underthing, her bangs limp and curling up, that even Casualty'd given up his roost on the couch and accompanied Artfag out, cos they were good roommates and knew not to interfere until things became way too damn depressing, and he'd actually met girls and now was seeing like two girls but he couldn't always remember which was which so sometimes when they came over he just let them talk and talk and talk and he smiled and finally he handed them the bong and one of them liked to smoke and the other one didn't and that's how he could finally remember which name to whisper during the sexings.

Casualty had mad respect for the gangas and thought about becoming a Rastafarian, but not in a white condescending or colonizing way.

& that is important to someone somewhere but not to the narrative at hand.

So, Homegirl was in her bedroom packing up a knapsack and whispering whispering to herself, & Casualty and Artfag were on the couch whispering, whispering.

And this was what Casualty & Artfag were whispering:

Casualty said, Dude.

Artfag took another bong hit and let it mellow and then exhaled and said, all coughy, Yes?

Casualty said, Gun?

Artfag said, So?

Casualty said, Homegirl?

Artfag said, Fucked up?

Yeah, said Casualty. But she's ours, said Casualty.

Yeah, said Artfag. But sometimes you gots to lets them go, said Artfag.

Casualty said, You believe that crap?

Artfag said, It ain't crap.

Casualty said, You gonna let Homegirl go?

Artfag said, I can.

Casualty said nothing.

Artfag, Can you let Homegirl go?

This is what Homegirl was whispering at the same time:

Homegirl said, Oh. Wow. Yes. Wow. Fuck. Fuck me. What. Fuck. Yes. No. What. What the fuck. Whatthefuck. What. The. Fuck.

Homegirl said, Fuckfuckfuckfuck. She tried to take a long breath. Then Homegirl said, What? & looked at Punkboy.

Punkboy'd let her get it all out.

177

Punkboy said, I was there and I waited for you.

But, Punkboy was not there; Punkboy was still pedaling pedaling. There was a fog, a creeping catting fog like his love and it was catnipping at his heels and his senses and he was zipping lopsided almost and he was zipping faster and faster and he didn't know where he was or where he was going.

Homegirl said, Yes. Somehow. I knew you were there, too.

Punkboy said, I saw his scooter. I cut the lights so you could escape.

Homegirl said, Deus ex machina.

Homegirl said, I shot my glock and then ran out.

Homegirl said, I might've killed someone.

Homegirl said, Fuck.

Punkboy said, Fuck.

Homegirl said, I'm so glad you were there.

Punkboy said, Me too.

Homegirl said, You saved my life.

Punkboy didn't say anything. What do you say to something like that? Instead he grabbed her and they kissed and kissed, standing there parallel and then they weren't parallel at all; they were kissing on the bed and the glock was on the nightstand so Homegirl could get as freaky as she wanted so they were sucking face and feeling each other's chests and breast and Homegirl's cunt was so wet and Punkboy's nice hard punk fingers were just figuring that out and Punkboy's cock was so hard and Homegirl's nice long homegirl fingers were just starting to play with that...

& the boys on the couch were still trying trying to decide what to do about Homegirl and the glock.

& is Homegirl actually rubbing one out at a time like this?

FORTY-THREE

& yeah, Shadow's gots Roomyakacraigslistwitch's gun now.

& no, Homegirl ain't rubbing one out. She's not even lying on the bed. She's standing in her bedroom & she's trying not to cry & she's trying to decide which way to fly.

& yeah, Roomyakacraigslistswitch's dead now, too.

Ding dong the witch is dead.

Which old witch?

Roomywitch.

& wouldn't it be something if Homegirl'd been rubbing one out as the po showed up to take her guilty ass in and then she'd be known as the masturbating murderess or some shit like that but in the neighborhood Homegirl lived in she'd have time to rub one out and clean up and buy herself roses and maybe even take herself out for tacos before the pos ever showed up. So, it'd never happen. Even if she had been.

FORTY-FOUR

Homegirl opened her window that led out to the front porch and she crawled through and then ran ran ran out of there. Homegirl ran out not cos she was running from the po tho she needed to be thinking the things about that soon soon. Homegirl ran cos she was done packing up her knapsack. Homegirl ran cos she'd just had a psychotic break where she was imagining making love to Punkboy, that Punkboy had somehow saved her from the shit that she was in before she even got in the shit. Homegirl was crying cos she'd just had that break and now she thought she loved Punkboy, and she was running cos she was afraid he felt the same way and he would try to find her.

Which is what for herself she wanted more than anything in the world. Which is what she didn't want for Punkboy cos she was afraid he'd get hurt or jailed or killed hanging with her.

What she wants for Punkboy is for him to grow old and happy with someone safe. All of a sudden, she wants for him life and safety and comfort and all the things she'd rejected all her life. The babies, the little Gap outfits, the jogging strollers, the espresso machine cos Punkboy and his lady'd been up all night with the babies and needed legal joltings before they dropped the chilluns off at daycare and went to work.

What she didn't know was that Punkboy wants only her up against all the garage doors of the world.

She ran and cried and knew better than to get in her car and drive anywhere cos now she was thinking about the po and knew the po might soon be looking for her. So she ran down the streets and it was like midnight, but she didn't leave behind any goddamned glass shoe and she had no idea what time it was, but somehow she knows it's not bartime and then she's outside this cream city brick triangular building and it sounds like a bar and it looks like a bar and it smells like a bar.

And she goes in.

FORTY-FIVE

Punkboy's still in the fog.

Punkboy's in the cat-fog of love and he is panic-pedaling.

Punkboy's not avoiding any of my obstacles now cos I'm not throwing any at him. I feel for his catnipped high crazy. His adrenaline that pumps him as he stands and pedals to get up hills switching gears yet still straining to push that bike forward through the fog and up and up and there are so many hills suddenly so many and he is sweating and he is exhausted and nothing seems to look familiar. There are no hoopdies and there are no dive bars and there are no former houses owned by po and there is no Homegirl. There is just a white blur and it is soft with a rough tongue and it licks Punkboy upside the head.

It says, Come to me.

It says, I am everything.

It says, Forget the world.

It says, Good luck, fucker.

Punkboy wishes for a sign and doesn't know where he is. Punkboy thinks, I will look for Homegirl at home. Punkboy thinks, I will not click my heels together. Punkboy thinks, Maybe, I will.

Punkboy keeps on standing and pushing and the hill keeps on hilling and all Punkboy can think about is Homegirl and how much trouble she's in by now cos it's hours since he left work and he's still ride-riding and finally he is panting and sweating and shaking and there it is all furry white fog-covered love, the end of the hill, and he gets to the end of the hill and there he can see through the fog and through the fog he can see at the bottom of the hill is a white dive bar and he knows that white dive bar. He is intimate with that dive bar. He has been intimate with Homegirl's pussy in the bathroom of that dive bar. He can coast to that white dive bar. Soon, he can coast for at least a minute and so he pumps hard harder.

It is not fate and it is not luck that he is there, but he knows where he is and where he's going and for Punkboy that's all that matters at this point.

That and the coasting.

FORTY-SIX

The sirens were finally sirening and the blue and red were flashing on the burning walls of Roomywitch's final abode and Homegirl musta felt this somewhere cos she ordered a purple haze and she didn't know why and she didn't even know where the name or thought of the drink'd come from in this weird little bar where she was the only customer and she could barely see the bartender's face; he kept turning it away from her and she was ignoring this and ignoring the fact she'd never heard his voice and when he wasn't serving her – only her – he was wiping glasses dry with a towel. Wiping wiping clean wet glasses dry. But who'd gotten them dirty? Why was there any need to dry them? There was no one there but Homegirl to make glasses dirty and to dry glasses for. He kept wiping those glasses dry but he didn't clean any. He had rows and rows of wet wet glasses to dry. They were lined up, dead but already cleaned little soldiers…orderly and shiny clean like military caskets sent home from the war.

She didn't think about any of this shit tho cos she'd just ordered a purple haze almost involuntarily and didn't know where she was or where she was going. Plus she didn't even like liqueurs. Even liqueurs made by Jim Beam. The bartender served it to her and it was purple and she couldn't see his face even tho she kept trying to and she drank the double shot down and shuddered and ordered whiskey on the rocks cos even tho those lights were still flashing flashing at the place where Richboy's body was burning she didn't know this and she couldn't take any more aftershocky shots.

FORTY-SEVEN

Punkboy finally knew where he was going and how to get there. Punkboy was pedaling pedaling to Homegirl's home.

He was at her house and so pumped he rode his bike up onto her porch. He was so pumped he didn't notice her open window. He was so pumped he dropped his bike and started banging on her door.

He wanted her to answer. He wanted Homegirl to answer the door in nothing but a clean merry widow. No, he wanted her to answer the door in nothing. Completely naked and flushed and waiting and ready.

Artfag answered the door.

Artfag said, Hi.

Punkboy said, Hi.

(I was still squeaky clean.)

Punkboy said, Homegirl in?

Artfag leaned in and whispered, She's gots a gun.

Fuck, Punkboy said and then pushed past Artfag. Artfag wasn't used to being treated like this; he was hipster royalty. Fuck yourself, man, he said.

Punkboy didn't hear him cos Punkboy was all thinking, What the fuck? A gun? and shit and so on…, but Casualty heard and Casualty was lurching himself up from the couch to protect his bro if he had to.

Punkboy knocked and knocked on Homegirl's door. He started thinking about what the gun was for and how she may have gone all vigilante by herself like he was afraid she would, which was why he hardly ever left her alone now and he should have just asked her and he should have just talked to her and now he wanted to blow shit up for reals, the bike ride through the fog and the drunk bitch who'd almost hit him with her car door and the crack/coke dive bar and that fucking hill and the coffeeshop and this day and this door above all else, and what if she was all fucked up from the vigilanting and she was in her room in the dark and she was crying and burning and she had that gun to her head. Punkboy started pounding on that door he wanted to blow up.

Artfag was behind him and yelling, Stop. What the fuck? Stop. Goddamn. & then Artfag was getting his cellie out to call the po cos Artfag'd had enough.

Then Casualty was behind him, too, and Casualty was saying, Punkboypunkboy.

& Punkboy was pounding and couldn't hear and the cheap plywood was starting to crack.

& Casualty put his hand on Punkboy's shoulder and said, Hey Punkboy!

Punkboy didn't hit Casualty cos even in his frantic pounding wanna blow up shit state he recognized the voice of his co-worker, his friend, the guy with the dank dank pot. Punkboy quit pounding.

Just turn it, Casualty almost whispered. Then he signaled Artfag to hang up before the 911 op answered.

Punkboy turned the doorknob.

The cracked door opened.

Homegirl was not there.

Punkboy sagged and then slid down to the floor. Casualty looked at Artfag and Artfag could tell that look meant, Get Ole Faithful. & even tho Artfag was hipster royalty this was trumped by Casualty's sweet kind center of his white Rastafarian self, his tootsie pop soul.

If anyone had a soul, it was Casualty and this was why the ladies were always always after him even when he fell asleep on them. They were safe with him; he would never butt rape or date rape or fuck them when they were dry...

Casualty grabbed the big bong from Artfag and held it to Punkboy's mouth and got the lighter positioned to light the dank buds up. Inhale, he said.

Punkboy shook his head.

You need this, Casualty said. You need it. Clear your head. It'll help you clear your head.

Punkboy thought about pushing the bong away, thought about throwing it against the wall, about blowing Ole Faithful up into little quarks of glass and gangas but he knew it wouldn't help; it wouldn't do anything but break Casualty's heart.

& that's all Casualty had left after the brain cells died out.

Then there was the lighting and the sucking and the gurgling and the blowing out and the three boys sat in a circle just inside Homegirl's room and it was dark cos none of them had thought to turn the light on and it was almost primal with the flames flickering and the damp dewy bud smell and their shadows dancing dancing on the wall.

Those shadows were not quite happy, but they were in communion.

FORTY-EIGHT

Homegirl was alone at the bar still and she was getting shitty.

Homegirl was alone drinking the whiskeys.

Homegirl was getting shitty and she was thinking sad thoughts to herself. She was thinking these thoughts about Punkboy and how bad she was for him and how she just brings trouble with her and pitying herself and that pity started turning into paranoia and she started to think she might be dead and that this triangular hole in the wall was hell and the bartender, well, she hadn't seen his face or heard his voice and all she could see were his big big hands wiping glasses dry and those hands were looking very familiar and she was having little flashback feelings of big hands on her face and big hands on her neck pushing her down, pushing her face into the bed and then turning her over and she can see the big hands and the big hands are moving down her body, from her neck to her pussy slowly and she's tied up and she can't move and all she can do is tingle and watch the hands sweep her body and watch them stop at her pussy, right outside her pussy, and then move back up and skirt her breasts and she's arching and she wants to be touched in those places, her tits are tingling and her pussy's nearly throbbing, but the big big hands are now moving down the sides of her waist, they're squeezing her tightly, they're holding her in and she's feeling this is so sexy and they move down to her pussy again and again they stop and the hands act like they'll do this all night and she knows they'll do this all night and it makes her so so wet and it makes her moan moan moan and she's about to come she thinks and the bartender says, You want it real bad, don't you?

The bartender says, You are a little bitch like all the other bitches.

FORTY-NINE

But... isn't Richboy dead, you say.

Yes. Don't worry. He's dead. His attitude isn't, tho. You can't kill an attitude like that with just one shot from a baby glock.

Duh.

His tude channels itself from warm male body to warm male body from Hamm's drinker to Pibber drinker to Stella drinker to scotch. His tude crushes the hearts of the women around the men it inhabits briefly. His tude walks the streetlit streets after bartime and finds crushed cigarette packs on the ground and picks them up and smokes the flattened smokes and doesn't care.

His tude wears a fedora low.

His tude's shoes are wearing thin.

His tude trips on sidewalk cracks and falls onto the grass and laughs and pisses and laughs.

His tude gets up and doesn't brush itself off and his tude's got a piss stain on its pants, but his tude don't care. His tude sees a porch it likes and hopes a woman lives there and knocks on the door and when a woman does answer, his tude tries to fuck and/or break up with her for fun.

Hopefully, Punkboy'll find Homegirl before anything happens. Or Homegirl'll stumble out of this weird little bar on her accord before anything happens between her and that bartender.

Or maybe the bartender's trying to get Homegirl to leave, so he can go do some blow or some meth or something cos boy keeps twisting twisting the towels around those glasses all ocdlike for no reason.

Or maybe the bartender's me and I'm trying to do the right thing – pushing that Homegirl right out the door, making her go look for her Punkboy. Maybe it's me and that right thing I'm doing is tinged with anger, which is why I say the mean Richboylike things. Anger I'm such a pussy and I can't make Homegirl love or even notice me. Anger she'll always love someone else no matter where or when I pop up. Anger that I'm a good person downdeep and want to do the right thing and wanting to do the right thing's seen as a weak thing which takes me right back to my first maybe.

Maybe Richboy started out like me – in love, in love, in love with the one who'll never love him back.

Or maybe I love Homegirl so much I only want what's best for her just like she does for Punkboy and if Punkboy doesn't really feel the same way about her I'm gonna smash a row of highball glasses upside his face til it's all blood-streaky and splintered and he looks like Richboy did before Richboy died.

Yep yep. That sounds about right.

FIFTY

Casualty said, Another round? He looked up at Punkboy. Punkboy was stoned and suddenly standing. Punkboy was kind of swaying. Or maybe that was just the light from the lighter flickering as Artfag hit the bong.

Punkboy said, Nah.

Casualty said, Go find her.

Artfag didn't say anything; he just sucked and the bong gurgled.

From the floor Casualty said, Find her. Tell her she can go home.

Punkboy turned and nodded. He shoulda been wearing a cowboy hat. He shoulda had a big Sam Elliot mustache he could tweak in farewell. He lifted his hand, tho, and saluted Casualty.

Casualty saw it waving in the flickering lighter light; Casualty saluted him back.

It was a touching man moment. The two men, concerned about their Homegirl. One in love with her, one not. Both pretty fucking stoned.

Punkboy turned and left.

That was the last time Casualty ever saw him.

FIFTY-ONE

Homegirl did stumble out of that weird triangular bar after seeing those big Richboy hands and feeling the feelings of them phantomlike on body parts that now she only wanted Punkboy to touch. She stumbled down the three stairs to the sidewalk and it was dark and it was quiet and she was in a part of the neighborhood she'd never been before so she got out her phone just in case and looked around. She saw an empty lumber yard and she saw duplexes and duplexes and there was a teeny playground down the block one way and the other way...

Railroad tracks.

She called Punkboy.

She said, Punkboy.

He said, Homegirl.

She said, It's me.

He said, Where are you?

She said, By the railroad tracks.

She said, Are you in?

He said, You don't even have to ask.

He said, I'm coming.

He said, Wait for me.

She said, I will wait for you. Always and forever.

He said, I will come for you. Always and forever.

& the rumble of a train could be heard in the distance. Coming closer but not too fast. Time enough for the forever and always lovers to jump on and take off to wherever and ever.

I saw it all happen. It went down just like that.

Meta knows the truth, tho. Meta always knows.

Meta is not a creepy creeper even if Meta talks about Meta in the third person.

Really. I'm not a creepy creeper. Really. Really.

& this is what happened...

They met up in the middle of the street and there was no one there and they kissed and kissed and the train was getting louder and the train horn was warning long and loud and they grabbed hands and they flew to the tracks, Homegirl gun-free and wobbly in her big boots and small skirt, Punkboy all stoned and shit, limping a bit after the panic-love-fogride, but both still flying flying. The train was slowing at the crossing and they still had each other's hands and there was an open door on a car somehow – I had nothing to do with that, no sir – and they looked at each other and smiled and they jumped into a future where they could figure out, like Punkboy wanted, all that man/woman stuff and love and life on their own.

& they held each other in the car as the train took them away and even tho it was night out and the darkness surrounded them, and tho that darkness surrounding them tried to pull them apart and tho that darkness tried to make Homegirl remember the ex-Marine & that spark of light cos that darkness was a tricky darkness & tho that darkness tried to make Punkboy remember waking up alone in post-concert parking lots, dark sky and grey fuzzed tongue, Homegirl and

Punkboy ignored that darkness and held each other tighter against it and said love things in each other's ears and that darkness knew it was beatdown for now and that darkness was sick of being left out in the cold so that darkness became a small baby that tried to cry but only coughed once and Homegirl and Punkboy didn't even hear it so lo, it crawled up between them and curled up with them forever and always for warmth.

They were warm and together and holding each other and hurtling hurtling across this land...

Meta is a hopeless romantic.

Meta wants this more than anything. That love wins out, even now.

Well, not more than anything. If Meta could make Homegirl love him, Meta would pop Punkboy with a glock two times quick.

& I hate to tell you this is not what happened.

& I hate to tell you someone keeps forgetting about Shadow.

FIFTY-TWO

Before the sirens could come sirening, Shadow set Roomy's house on fire and then creeped out.

Before the sirens of po and fire trucks showed up, Shadow chucked his open, lit zippo on the bodies of Roomywitch & Richboy, & then creeped out onto the streets of Riverwest. Shadow met up with the darkness on the streets and Shadow stopped the creepy creeping. Shadow got bigger and balder as he joined with the darkness; Shadow's neck rolls got harder and bigger and twingier. Shadow joined with the darkness on the streets and now he lumbered lumbered.

Shadow was now a part of the darkness; Shadow was following the darkness. Shadow was following the trail of Homegirl's pussy through the darkness. Shadow could see it shimmering in the darkness and it was pointing him east and it was lighting up the darkness vaguely. On the periphery.

Shit was gonna go down, Shadow and the darkness thought.

Or maybe Shadow said that to the darkness.

Or maybe it was just a promise.

Maybe this is the crossroads.

FIFTY-THREE

Homegirl was still in that weird bar. She hadn't left, even after the bartender said what he said. She couldn't stop watching his hands. She watched them as she drank and she watched them as she waited for another drink and she watched them as she sat there and smoked and she watched them.

She had forgotten all about the cops and all about the running and all about what she should or should not be doing with Punkboy.

The bartender hadn't said anything to her since the little bitch comment. He knew he didn't need to. He just kept the drinks coming. He started choosing her drinks cos he could tell she wasn't paying attention. He could tell her fascination. He was good like that.

Homegirl was sipping a bourbon & feeling fascinated & feeling fine. She was watching the hands and the hands were drying and the hands were flying and the hands were reminding. They were reminding her of hands on her. Hands on her and the last hands she'd had on her were Punkboy's. She started thinking little things about Punkboy. Even through the fascination.

Or maybe because of the fascination. The hands were drying drying. & Homegirl started thinking about Punkboy. About the death metal soundtrack to his life. About pint glasses smashing & his delicate boy wrists. There were sometimes pint glasses smashed at work and there was often death metal at close and there were always Punkboy's wrists. & every now & then, Homegirl'd been afraid that Punkboy'd stick his delicate boy wrists into the sudsy water or the rinsing water now full of the sudsing water and come up surprised bleeding wrists from a smashed pint glass submersed in suds.

She started thinking about how he was so skinny & how he had a big cyst on his back in the middle of his huge tattoo & how he once had a shitstache & how he'd dated that chick when she'd gone away even when he'd always liked her, Homegirl knew, & yet had never made that mad move on her.

& was that what love was?

& was she gonna start sounding like fucking Tina Turner or some shit?

Homegirl'd rather have the steamy windows. & the rain.

She started thinking about his primavera & that wasn't a euphemism. & could he make anything besides primavera? & could she listen to his punk rock & his death metal foreverandever as they were getting it on?

He'd taken her to the doctor.

He'd cared so much for her.

Punkboy'd cared so much for her she'd been hoping he'd be gone when she got out of the doctor's office, when she came back to that mutant ninja turtle lounge. The bright orange plastic chairs. The buzzing in door. The judgy bitch. She was hoping it'd be just her and judgy bitch cos she coulda taken on judgy bitch. She coulda grabbed her through that little money divet under the plastic window; she coulda grabbed the bitch's throat & crushed her windpipe. Or at least screamed in her face & then head-butted the bitch to concussion. Empty womb & tears & all... But, when she saw Punkboy sitting there, waiting, Homegirl knew.

Doomed, she was doomed.

It was why she hadn't pop-popped the glock right after that workshop. It was part of the reason why she'd been all bloody merrywidowing sleep sleep sleeping.

That & the unbabies.

The unbabies looked like Punkboy, in her daydreams. While she laid there on her dirty bed, in her bloody merry widow. The unbabies skateboarded & flipped & dmxed & fixied & every now and then would break a nose or a delicate wrist, or a pit bull would come running up at a skateboarding unbaby & Homegirl'd hafta flick that motherfucking pit right off her stomach & Homegirl'd known, even in her fucked-up state & merry widow, that this was all revery; & Homegirl'd known this was how she'd act if anyone ever fucked with any of hers.

She'd wipe those motherfucking pit bulls out with her bare hands if she had to.

She'd grab them by their face and unlock their locklocking jaws.

She would do anything to keep hers safe.

It would be so much work.

So much more work than the foodservicing or the schooling or even the writing.

So much goddamned work. & Homegirl was feeling kinda tired already. Homegirl was thinking maybe she should go back to merry widowing and sleep sleeping.

Homegirl watched the bartender's hands wiping & those fingers were not as thick or as dexterous as Punkboy's & those wrists were not as delicate as his, either.

Homegirl'd watched Punkboy cleaning pint glasses at work. She'd watched him wash dishes at his home. She'd watched him clean; she'd never offered to help. She'd never gotten past the bedroom to imagine anything more.

She didn't know anything more.

Homegirl was beginning to wonder, as she watched the bartender's white, flighty hands, what it would be like. To wash the dishes with someone else. To own dishes. To own dishes with someone else and have to take care of them. To take on things and take care of them. To take care of things. She was at a bar. She knew this. She'd just killed someone. She knew this, too. She couldn't take care of things.

She couldn't take care of herself. Let alone babies.

Or even unbabies.

The bartender put a tall pour of cheap pinot noir in front of Homegirl. My treat, he said. Like I said, it was the first thing he'd said to her in a while.

Then he said, Something to eat? We have a special tonight…primavera.

His tongue flitted over his lips and he looked like Shadow for a sec how Shadow looked when there were two girls with guns or whenever he thought about Homegirl's shimmering cunt.

Homegirl didn't catch it but maybe she should have. Maybe she would've been more prepared…

& maybe he overplayed his hand; maybe he got too cocky. Homegirl stopped staring at his hands and stared into the dark red of the wine. She licked her lips; she trembled a bit. For some reason she felt like Snow White or some shit in the forest with the woodsman who sets her free; she was excited and a little wet like they don't tell you Snow White was. Alone in the forest with a man who could snap her neck just like that. Just cos someone told him to. Just cos she was who she was.

She took a sip. She looked at the bartender's thick wrists. She thought of Punkboy's delicate wrists. Then said, I killed a man today.

The bartender stopped wiping glasses. His hands fell to his sides like birds or something. Like bicycles, like does taken before their first rut. He was vaguely surprised and irritated.

Homegirl looked into the pinot again. I may have to kill another, she said and began swirling her glass.

I may have to cut out his heart, she whispered. I will have to put his heart in a box, she thought.

The bartender's hands started flapping on their own accord like they were trying to fly away. The bartender grabbed two bar rags and started wiping down the bar to keep Homegirl from seeing.

He had overplayed his hand. He had overplayed his hand & Richboy's tude left him & Richboy's tude was hovering, glistening in the dark bar air.

FIFTY-FOUR

Punkboy jumped back on that bike & was pedaling again.

He was pedaling through the Riverwest streets looking for Homegirl again. This time he was pedaling through any obstacle. This time he was jumping & twisting & not stopping.

This time he knew Homegirl had a gun.

This time he knew someone was or soon would be dead.

And while he was pedaling, Shadow was lumbering. Shadow was lumbering and following the shimmer. Lumbering Shadow was the three wise men in one. Shadow was the three wise men & instead of myrhh or gold or hippiescent, Shadow was bringing a motherfucking gun.

Turning and turning are Punkboy's wheels.

Lumbering and lumbering is Shadow's bulk.

Riverwest's all quiet except for the drunks and the crazies and the homeless rooting through bins for leftover sushi & PBR dregs.

The drunks are sounding through the dark like foghorns.

The Homegirl cannot hear the Shadower.

Homegirl is still thinking fairy-tale, still thinking Snow White and the bartender's a dwarf and there'll be a prince soon and a kiss.

Little does she know it's more like there'll be a prince and stepsisters cutting off their own toes & cooking them up and serving them with bloody tea while bleedingbleeding all over the fucking place for a chance at wedded bliss.

Something's slouching towards Bethlehem or some shit.

Shadow saw the faint glowing in the East and he followed it. Punkboy had no guide, no angel, nothing and he rode his bike up and down the streets.

Of course, Punkboy's gonna run into lumbering Shadow.

Who could possibly miss or forget him?

FIFTY-FIVE

Punkboy saw Shadow and started following him.

There was a triangular building just up the block and to Shadow it was shimmering and to Punkboy it was a building he didn't take much notice of cos he was too busy trying to be all surreptitious on his fixie. He was pedaling quietly, slowly in the shadows of Shadow.

Shadow stopped just outside the triangular building. He inhaled deeply. He mighta drooled. To Shadow that weird triangular building smelled like a cunt and looked like a cunt and he was gonna rip that cunt open.

Punkboy could tell Shadow was gonna go in. Punkboy could just tell. He pedaled fastfast and skidded in front of Shadow. Before Shadow could pull his gun, Punkboy'd picked his fat fixie up. Punkboy'd thrown it on him.

Punkboy thought he could get in and out before Shadow got up.

Punkboy thought maybe the bar'd have a back exit.

Punkboy thought, The bartender would be on the side of love.

The bartender was still wiping the bar down and Homegirl was still feeling all Snow White huntress heart in a box when Punkboy stormed in.

Punkboy stormed in, followed by a lumbering Shadow.

Did Punkboy really think his fixie would slow down obsessed mercenary cunt sniffing Shadow?

If only Shadow'd lumbered in first, maybe things would have gone down differently. If only Punkboy hadn't tried to save Homegirl again, maybe. Maybe Homegirl & Punkboy'd be on that train right now hurtling through the darkness of the US & that darkness'd be coo-cooing at their feet. But Punkboy came in first and Punkboy was the first to go.

Have I overplayed my hand?

When Homegirl saw Punkboy, her heart felt like it should go in the box. She whispered, Punkboy. Punkboy didn't hear cos then there was lumbering Shadow and Homegirl was all of a sudden jumping out of her bar stool and pulling her glock free from her cleavage and sending her pinot hurling at the bartender and the wine glass was shattering all over the bar – shimmering shimmering – and the pinot was oilslicking the two white bird hands and the bartender was transfixed like Homegirl had been and then Punkboy was caught up in Shadow's big hairless arm and then Shadow had a gun to Punkboy caught in a headlock and Punkboy was having Bigbrother flashbacks and he was wishing he was a bomb and he could explode and take Shadow out and save Homegirl once and for all and Homegirl somehow knew this thought and for Homegirl this was just too much.

She said, Shoot Punkboy. Fuck.

She said, See what I care.

She said, I'm done with him.

She said, I'm done with all of them. & she pointed at the bartender who was looking at his wine-red hands still. Still, he was and looking looking within.

Richboy's tude hung there glistening, waiting to see who

would win this time.

Richboy's tude was learning not to always bet against Homegirl.

Richboy's tude was learning…

Shadow said, I know you, bitch.

Shadow squeezed on Punkboy's neck a little. Punkboy tried not to cough. Shadow squeezed more. Punkboy coughed and it almost sounded like a frog croaking. Richboy's tude smiled and shimmered. The darkness waited. Shadow squeezed harder. Punkboy's breath went a little jagged; Punkboy's breath went soft and Homegirl heard it; Homegirl felt it. Homegirl felt it like a dagger and felt it like velvet and felt it like her heart cut out by a woodsman's deft hand and then a heart placed in a velvet-lined box.

Homegirl knew she had to stop this; Homegirl didn't know how to stop it.

FIFTY-SIX

Homegirl had to prove it and so Homegirl shot Punkboy.

Homegirl shot Punkboy.

Twice actually.

Before Homegirl shot Punkboy, she stood there with her glock and Shadow was squeezing Punkboy & Homegirl knew she was the reason he would die and she couldn't take that responsibility and so she looked behind her and there was that bartender and his white dove now red hands waving and she pulled back the trigger and this is what Homegirl wanted to have happen.

Pop went her glock and then one of his hands went flying. Solo.

The bartender screamed and there was bloodblood and it was like the reverse of those stepsisters. Cos his finger would never have fit that ring, yo. The bartender kept screaming and his solo hand landed with a flop on the bar by itself and it seemed to do a little death rattle and its partner was waving wildly wildly, mated for life and delirious with grief.

All three of the men were fascinated. They all stared.

& then Shadow disappeared just like that. Poof gone. & Punkboy was free & coasting coasting to her & then it was Punkboy & her kissing kissing & the bartender screaming & Richboy's tude glowering not glistening.

But that's not how it went down cos all Homegirl's gots is her little glock. & the laws of physics ain't gonna break themselves for her. The laws of physics ain't gonna be broke.

Broken.

Pop went her glock and pop went a couple of fingers and a spray of flesh & gristle & blood all over the bar & it was a mess & no bar rag alone could clean that shit up.

The bartender howling howling without stopping.

Bartender howled cos he was in pain & he was in shock & he couldn't begin to understand what'd just happened or how things could've gone so wrong.

Richboy's tude, hovering and glistening, laughing.

Tude laughed cos this shit was so funny.

Shadow squeezed on Punkboy nearstrangling.

Bartender bled and howled & bled some more. Bartender said, Help me.

Shadow didn't help, but you know that. Shadow was too much enjoying the feel of Punkboy delicate neck tendon and ligaments under his fingers. Shadow was too much enjoying the power of his own digits. Shadow wouldn't have helped anyway cos that's how Shadow roll.

But you already know...

Punkboy couldn't help cos he was trying to somehow survive beneath Shadow's big manhands.

Homegirl didn't help cos she was caught between some kind of weird shame spiral for all of this shit – Punkboy's life in Shadow's hands, literally, & also cos she was the asshole that shot the bartender.

Homegirl thought, Well, he's a creepycreeper bartender.

Homegirl thought, He kinda deserves it.

Homegirl thought, Not really.

Homegirl thought, Ever heard of a fucking tourniquet.

Homegirl thought, You gotta free hand.

& then Homegirl laughed.

Homegirl laughed because none of this was funny.

Homegirl laughed cos all of it was too funny.

Homegirl laughed and Shadow recognized something in it.

Shadow recognizing something, loosened his grip enough for Punkboy to say, Help him.

Shadow, savoring that thing like it was his neck twinge or Homegirl's desperation, loosened his grip some more.

Punkboy said, Just help him then you & me up against all the garages. Homegirl! You and me…

But, Homegirl turned her gun on Punkboy and Shadow started squeezesqueezing again. Homegirl turned her gun on Punkboy and started thinking, Unbabies.

Homegirl thought, I am tired.

Homegirl thought, How can I take care?

Homegirl thought, Why should I?

Homegirl thought, Why me?

& it was so random. Just like everything in her life.

Homegirl trained her gun on Punkboy and took careful aim.

Homegirl shot Punkboy in the shoulder, but Shadow didn't let him go and Punkboy didn't fall fall from the impact onto the dirty bar floor.

The bartender watched it all still screaming & his hand holding his other hand waving wild bird shadow puppets & shit.

Homegirl didn't know what to do.

Homegirl trained her glock on Shadow next.

Homegirl said, You still want me?

Shadow squeezed Punkboy's neck a bit tighter in accord. Poor Punkboy was shot and being strangled and there was no end in sight.

Homegirl knew this. Homegirl tried to turn Shadow's attention to her. Homegirl said, Try and get me.

Then Homegirl said, Come and get me.

Shadow didn't move except to squeeze Punkboy more. Punkboy's shoulder bled; Punkboy's face got purpler.

Homegirl said, I've got a box and it's looking for a heart & mama don't care which one of you she's gots to cut down.

Then Homegirl shot her glock again.

& then.

& then Homegirl took up her glock & her box & her heart and stepped away from that mess & went back out.

There was no screen door slamming.

& only the darkness followed.

Please review this book, and help support the
author and independent publishing. Thank you.